GRIFFIN '96

LOST IN LOVE

"Would you kiss me?" Lark asked Nathan.

If he kissed her, it would be more than a kiss. There was more involved here than lips touching lips. There were souls involved. And that scared him.

"Do you want to?"

He groaned. "God, yes."

"Then do it."

Her lips were the sweetest of invitations.

"I want to know how it feels."

He had a pretty good idea how it would feel.

But nothing he'd ever known prepared him for the seductive feel of her lips under his. She was all trembling, swollen softness. She was a delicate, quivering breath against his lips. She was the flutter of life deep within his lonely soul.

He had every right to be afraid.

————————

AMERICAN DREAMER

Theresa Weir

HarperPaperbacks
A Division of HarperCollinsPublishers

HarperPaperbacks
A Division of HarperCollinsPublishers
10 East 53rd Street, New York, N.Y. 10022-5299

ISBN: 0-06-108461-1

HarperCollins®, 🔥®, HarperPaperbacks™, and
HarperMonogram® are trademarks of HarperCollinsPublishers.

Cover illustration by Jim Griffin

First printing: May 1997

Printed in the United States of America

Visit HarperPaperbacks on the World Wide Web at
http://www.harpercollins.com

❖ 10 9 8 7 6 5 4 3 2 1

*In loving memory of my husband Bill,
who was, and continues to be,
an inspiration to us all. I hope you're
somewhere with a lot of trees.*

*Thanks for answering my tedious questions
about tractors. And animals. And electric fencing.
And thanks for coaching the kids in shock technique.
Over the years, it has added an entertaining
dimension to sibling rivalry.*

1

The land fell away from the plow blades in shiny, black, symmetrical waves. Released heat rose from the opened earth.

The ancient tractor rolled over the ground with the jarring impact of a physical assault, each bump sending renewed and invigorating signals to the pain center in Nathan Senatra's head.

Plowing would be a helluva lot easier without a hangover.

He couldn't believe he'd let himself get so damn drunk. Normally he didn't drink, at least not for the sole purpose of getting loaded. But last night, for some reason, despair and loneliness had settled in his belly like a stone, and he'd found himself seeking numbness at the local tavern.

He should have gone to bingo at the VFW instead. Better yet, he should have exhibited a little self-control. Now he couldn't even remember how he'd gotten home. A scary thing, to misplace ten hours of your life. He'd not only found the numbness he'd been seeking, but total oblivion as well.

He straightened in the tractor seat, trying to relieve the ache in his lower back.

No good.

He groaned. His thirty-two-year-old body felt at least seventy.

The field was fifty acres—small by Iowa standards, but when you were pulling a two-bottom chisel plow with a widow-maker tractor that couldn't even be sold as scrap metal, a job that shouldn't have taken more than an afternoon was going to turn into forty-eight hours of eating dirt.

The widow-maker—or donor tractor, to which it was also affectionately referred—was one of the few things left after the divorce settlement. Nathan figured leaving it to him had been wishful thinking on Mary Jane's part.

The 748 model, with its small front wheels and high center of gravity, had only been in production for six months. After it had tipped and crushed several of its owners, the company wisely trashed the design and started over. A year later, they admitted defeat and closed up shop.

Nathan tried to tell himself he should admit defeat and move on. Learn a new skill. Get a job in town.

But for some reason, he couldn't let go.

There had been a time when working the land, when raising a nice herd of cattle had meant everything to him. But now . . . now farming was fast becoming a burden.

It was hard to stick around when something you loved was in danger of becoming something you hated.

It wasn't just the divorce and the fact that his vision of

a contented life had soured. As the years passed, he became more and more of an outsider, even among other farmers. Especially among other farmers.

His neighbors said he was crazy because he left brush and grass strips for wildlife. Instead of cutting down trees, he planted around them.

Maybe they had something. Maybe he *was* crazy. Every day of his life was like fighting World War III with a plastic sword.

He didn't have a chance. No way could he stop the devastation.

When he reached the top of a gentle rise, he put in the clutch, shifted to neutral, and decreased the engine's speed, letting the tractor roll to a stop. He stood, legs braced apart, and worked his fingers into the sweat-damp front pocket of his jeans. He pulled out four soggy, none-too-clean aspirin, briefly contemplated them in a none-too-clean palm, then tossed them in his mouth. He grabbed his thermos from behind the tractor seat, the container's lack of weight reminding him it was empty.

"Shit."

He wedged the thermos back where it had been, quickly chewed and swallowed the bitter pills. Then he sat down, reached into his shirt pocket, and pulled out a few sunflower seeds. He popped them in his mouth, the salty hulls quickly killing the bitter taste left by the aspirin.

To his left was ground he used to own. It now belonged to his ex and it made his blood boil whenever he looked at it—usually several times a day. She not only owned something that had been in his family for generations, she'd stripped it bare.

Raped his dream.

The bitch had wiped out every tree, every blade of grass. She'd even torn down the two-story farmhouse where he'd grown up, and put in a double-wide trailer, all done out of spite because he'd been the dump*er* while she'd been the dump*ee*.

Head pounding with every beat of his heart, Nathan let his gaze pan to the right, down the hill, past the pond and cattle, to the tenant house that was now his permanent residence. It wasn't bad during the hot months, but in winter it was ruthless. With the woodstove cranked all the way up, he couldn't keep the place above fifty degrees.

As he watched, waiting for his head to stop throbbing, he saw a car turn up his lane.

White. Relatively new. One of those little foreign jobs.

Probably another bill collector. Or a salesman.

Nobody he wanted to see.

He put in the clutch, put the tractor in gear, increased the engine speed, and continued on his way.

It took about fifteen minutes to reach the end of the field. He automatically lifted the plow blades, turned, sank the blades into the ground, and headed back.

For a moment he wondered if he was hallucinating. Coming across the field was a woman with long, billowing hair the color of summer wheat. She was so far away that her outline was indistinct, the colors blending with the heat waves rising from the ground.

He stopped and cut the engine.

As he watched her approach, he was dimly aware of the numbness in his hands caused by the vibration of the tractor. He ran a tongue across lips that tasted of dirt.

When she was close enough, she stopped and looked up at him, shading her face with one hand.

She wore a peach-colored sweater and a long skirt made out of material so soft that the wind molded it to her thighs. Her shoes were brown leather, the kind that just slipped on. And they were caked with dirt and mud.

All she needed was a sign that said, Out of My Element.

"Could you tell me where I can find Nathan Senatra?" she asked, shouting up at him. Her voice, under the noise of the wind, was cultured. City. Like somebody who'd taken lessons to learn to talk that way.

One hand on the wheel, the other on the back of the tractor seat, Nathan levered himself to his feet, then jumped.

He'd forgotten all about his headache. As soon as the soles of his workboots hit the ground, pain knifed through his skull. Fireworks flashed behind his eyes.

Wind stirred his flannel shirt, and he felt a hint of coolness where his back had been pressed against the tractor's black leather seat for so long. He hooked his thumbs in the belt loops of his jeans and hitched up his pants, all the while the woman-girl watching him with a strange sort of reluctant fascination.

He rubbed his bristly chin, remembering that he hadn't shaved in several days. Giving himself time to assess the situation, he took off his cap, wiped his forehead with the sleeve of his shirt, then replaced the cap. "Nathan Senatra, you say?"

She nodded.

He got a whiff of her perfume, or soap, or shampoo, or whatever. Light. Clean. He marveled at her mermaid's hair. He marveled at how out of place she looked in the middle of his field. And then he noticed that she was holding an official-looking folded leather case.

Was the mermaid here to serve him papers? What more could Mary Jane get out of him?

"Nathan Senatra," she repeated. "Do you know him?"

"Oh yeah."

He gave it some thought. Or at least pretended to. Then with his best hillbilly drawl, added, "Haven't seen him in some time."

She frowned and chewed her bottom lip. "Oh."

"But if I run into him, would you like me to give him a message?" He congratulated himself on his quick thinking, hangover and all.

"Mr. Senatra is signed up to participate in a federally funded contented farm animal study."

He made a choking sound. "I'm *what*?" He dropped the phony accent. He dropped all pretension of being someone else.

"I take it you're Mr. Senatra." In a smooth voice, she calmly continued, calmly explained. "It's a study to monitor the contentment of your cows."

Shit.

He tried to think, tried to figure out what was going on. The effort was too much. Blinding pain knifed through his head.

She opened her leather folder and started sifting through papers. "It was all arranged by a Mr. Nelson, from the Bank of Elizabeth."

Aha. Nelson. The loan officer. The study probably paid something, and Nelson knew Nathan was in danger of losing what little ground he had left. Nelson meant well, but he was an idiot.

As harmless as the girl looked, she had the power to close his cattle operation with a few lines jotted down in her notebook. Someone who couldn't pour piss from a boot had his life in her hands.

He had to get rid of her. Upset her so much she'd leave a trail of dust in her hurry to get away from him.

"My name is Lark. Lark Leopold."

He looked at the hand she'd extended, then crossed his arms over his chest. "Lark." He let a couple of seconds go by. "Is that your stage name?" He watched as shock waves of disgust rolled through her. "Or is that Lark, like someone who enjoys having a good time, regardless of the consequences?"

Lark lowered the hand he'd refused to take and closed her mouth, which she was sure had been hanging open in the most vacant way. She'd never encountered such rudeness. And he wasn't finished yet.

"The government has its nose in everything. Next thing you know, they'll be telling me when I can make love."

Heat flooded her cheeks. "This isn't an investigation." She hadn't expected hostility. She'd been led to believe that the participants had signed up of their own free will. "It's a study."

"I don't want you snooping around, sticking your nose in my business. I don't want to be under anybody's microscope." His gaze moved over her, taking in her city shoes and her city skirt and her city sweater and her city complexion. "Especially yours."

When he'd first jumped down from the tractor, he'd almost taken her breath away, he was that good-looking. His movements, as he'd swung himself to the ground, had been fluid, lithe, his muscles evident beneath his flannel shirt and faded jeans.

Her initial impression had been of a man who seemed a strange combination of rugged outdoors and vulnerable sensuality.

He had a nice, straight nose. The dark stubble on his face couldn't hide the flat planes where cheekbones met jaw. He had a mouth that was somewhat full, the corners curved in a disturbingly sexy way.

And his eyes. Blue, blue, blue. Intelligent. Penetrating. Direct.

She was wondering why the good-looking ones were so often jerks, when he blasted her again.

"What are your qualifications? Have you studied animal behavior?"

She would say she was getting a good example of it now.

"Animal husbandry? Animal health?" He pulled in a breath, and forged on. "You don't have any, do you?"

She raised her chin. "The job description required keen observation skills. I could relate my observations regarding your manners, but I'm not that rude. Instead, it's enough for you to know that I've been employed by a private research firm for the last several years." She didn't think it necessary to mention that her employer had been her father.

"Ah." He gave a slow, knowing nod. "Desk job." Without waiting for a reply, he continued, his voice thick with sarcasm. "Spend too much time in a situation like that, you lose touch with reality. People stagnate in that kind of artificial environment."

She pressed her leather case against her stomach, crossing her arms tightly over it.

"Did you come here for fun, like going to a foreign country to gawk at the natives?"

She thought he was finished, but apparently he was only getting warmed up. "Who are you to come here when you know nothing about farming or livestock, so you can put together your little study and take your summer vacation." He placed a splayed hand to his chest. "This is my life. My *life.*"

He pointed at her. "Get off my property. Stay the hell away from my livestock."

Before he decided to carry her off bodily, she swung around, folder in hand, and marched away.

Lark tried to move with some dignity, knowing the man was probably watching her, but it was hard to be graceful on uneven ground. She lost a shoe and had to hobble back two steps to retrieve it. As she slid her foot in place, balancing with her arms outstretched, she realized her legs were trembling.

What a disgusting man. Was that the way men were here? Did it have something to do with spending so much time outdoors? Did it make them regress?

What was so demoralizing was the fact that he was right. She hardly knew a cow from a cat. An udder from a . . . from a . . . tail. A teat from a tat. And she *had* thought the job would be fun. What was wrong with that? It had also been a chance to strike out on her own in a way that wasn't permanent. She loved her parents, but they had sheltered her for far too long. And she'd let them, taking comfort in the security they so willingly provided.

Somewhere along the line, time had gotten away from her. Weeks had turned into months, months to years. One day she suddenly realized she was thirty years old and living with her parents. It was past time to shake things up, to let go and try the world again. She just hadn't known the world was going to include somebody like Nathan Senatra.

At least she'd exhibited a modicum of self-control— something that couldn't be said for him. At least she'd refrained from picking up a dirt clod and throwing it at his head.

A clod for a clod.

When she was opposite the pasture with the cows she'd seen earlier, she looked over her shoulder. From her location, she couldn't see the tractor, only hear it.

The engine labored. A puff of exhaust drifted on the horizon.

Until she was told differently, she had a job to carry out, she thought, assuring herself that her obstinacy had absolutely nothing to do with the rudeness of the man on the tractor.

It took her a while to locate a gate. Or a sort of gate. It was constructed of three strands of barbed wire held in place by three perpendicular posts. Couldn't the man have a normal gate? With hinges and a latch?

To her disgust, she found she couldn't open it.

It looked as if she had three choices.

Over. Under. Through.

Through it was.

As she fought her way between the two lower strands, she thought about how the word "farmer" had taken on a whole new meaning. It was a word she no longer associated with warm flannel and soft, cuddly sheep. Now it ranked up there with battery acid. Poison ivy. Stomach flu.

One thing for sure, Nathan Senatra wasn't the friendly, polite PBS farmer she'd envisioned welcoming her to farm country with a hefty handshake and an endearing, Howdy, how ya doin'? He didn't even *look* like a farmer was supposed to look. He was more grunger than farmer. More brooding Heathcliff than warm and puppy-friendly Pat Boone. More dark gothic than American gothic.

Where were his bib overalls? His pitchfork? His stern-looking wife with the hair parted in the middle?

Did he have a wife? If so, she pitied the poor woman.

Barbed wire caught the back of her sweater. Barbed wire attacked her skirt. Muttering under her breath, she leaned closer to the ground, unhooking her sweater. Finally inside the pasture, feeling as if she'd just stormed Stalag 13, she tugged at her skirt, ripping the hem.

Skirt hem dragging the ground, her brown slip-ons weighted with mud, she made her way across the soft, bumpy ground.

With a pond as their backdrop, the cows looked up at her with soft, long-lashed eyes, dismissed her as harmless, then went back to munching grass.

The calves . . . they were *darling*. They played and jumped around as if they had springs on their feet, as if they were so full of joy they couldn't contain themselves.

Enchanted, Lark forgot all about her job. She even forgot about her unpleasant encounter with Mr. Farmer.

Birds called. Bees moved through the grass, from dandelion to dandelion. The sun, falling warm on her head, penetrating the back of her sweater, made her feel drowsy.

Clouds moved overhead. Once in a while, when the wind direction shifted, she caught a whiff of a scent she associated with greenhouses. A rich, peat kind of smell.

Almost paradise.

Near the center of the pond, a fish splashed. She watched the ripple fan out, finally making its way to shore.

Something was floating there, at the water's edge.

She stepped closer.

Something in the water.

She stepped closer still.

Something blue.

Cloth?

Something like a floating cloud of dark hair.

Something like an arm, with fingers gently undulating in the rippling water.

Lark let out a bloodcurdling scream and jumped back, catching the low heel of her shoe on a clump of grass, staggering, almost falling over backward.

Cattle scattered like a flock of landbound birds. Bellowing, they ran with awkward, stiff-legged gaits. The calves, unhindered by bulk, shot past their mothers like frantic, panic-stricken bullets.

Lark's mind alternately raced and stalled out completely.

A body.

In the water.

The cattle she was there to study, running rampant, sent into a berserk frenzy because of her scream.

Nothing in her life, nothing in the brief field-study seminar, certainly nothing in those years spent tucked away in her father's library, had prepared her in any way for this.

A body.

No.

She stared, her mind denying what her eyes saw.

From behind came a sound, a rustling.

She cried out, jumped, and swung around.

Nathan Senatra was striding toward her through the grass, an even deeper scowl on his face than he'd had before.

"Mr. Senatra! Am I glad to see you!"

And she was. Ten minutes ago, she'd despised the man. Now she adored him. She adored the way he hadn't shaved. Adored the capable way he walked. His take-charge attitude.

He stopped a few feet from her, his dusty, booted feet planted firmly on the ground, hands on his hips, the tails of his untucked flannel shirt flapping at his thighs.

"There seems to be a problem here—" she began. Her voice was high. Minnie Mouse on helium.

"The problem is, you're scaring the hell out of my cattle!"

He'd dropped the good ol' boy routine. His accent was as pure as someone from California.

"I can't believe you're actually getting paid to come here and raise hell. Don't you know how to act around livestock? Have you ever even *seen* a cow before?"

"Yes. No." From a distance. And in books. "Yes." She couldn't make herself look toward the body, but she pointed.

Puzzled, he followed the direction of her shaking finger, finally getting the message that there was more going on here than a few unhappy bovines.

"Son of a—"

He raced to the bank, the soles of his leather boots slipping on the mud and wet grass.

Lark turned away, her ears intent on every sound, every splash, her mind conjuring up images most likely as horrible as the real thing.

"Oh my God."

His whisper of stunned disbelief wasn't meant for her.

She turned slightly, so she could see him out of the corner of her eye.

He stood in the water, bent over, unmoving. Not a sound now, except for the birds calling overhead and the occasional bellow of a cow as the cattle calmed down, as mamas searched for their babies.

Then he straightened and came toward her, his shoulder

blocking whatever there was to see that she didn't want to see.

Her eyes found his—and stayed there. His irises were that startling blue. Her father had once shown her a cat-bird egg the same deep shade.

"D-dead?"

A foolish question, but one she had to ask.

He passed a hand over his face. "Yeah." Still stunned.

She let out a shaky breath. What had she expected? For him to tell her that some kid had thrown a dummy into the pond? That it was a sick, practical joke?

She found herself wondering if she should make reference to the body in her report, if it bore any significance to her study.

She'd never seen a dead body. Well, she'd been to her share of funerals, but the people always looked asleep. Not really dead. What was weird was that sometimes they bore no resemblance to the person you knew in life. And sometimes they looked even better.

"You're not going to faint, are you?"

It was more of an accusation than a question. They really put out the welcome mat here. Good old Midwestern hospitality. And then she remembered just what he'd said to her earlier. Pleasure without worrying about the consequences. Stage name. People often made fun of her name, but his comments were new ones.

He was watching her closely, and it occurred to her that his face, beneath the dirt and beard stubble, was extremely pale.

"It's Lark. Like the bird."

She knew what she was doing. Trying to take her mind away from the horror of the moment.

It worked for him. Some of his color came back.

Then, diverted like a crying toddler offered a piece of candy, he demanded, "Why the hell would somebody name you after a bird?"

"My father is an ornithologist."

He let out a loud snort.

Oh well. Like she'd always said whenever someone made fun of her name—at least her father's favorite bird wasn't the booby.

A body.

In the water.

It was no good. She couldn't quit thinking about it. Lark swallowed and thought about the next step. "Hadn't we better call the police?"

Confusion clouded his eyes. His color got bad again. And it suddenly occurred to her that he looked as if *he* might pass out.

He rubbed his head, knocking his cap to the ground. "I don't know," he said vaguely.

"I think that's the thing to do."

"Yeah. Yeah, I guess so."

He bent down and retrieved his cap. His hair was dark, and damp from perspiration, and as unkempt as the rest of him.

"Did you know the"—she almost said body—"person?"

He swallowed, replacing his cap once more. His Adam's apple moved up and down. Then came two words. A name. Spoken in a croak. "Mary Jane."

"Mary Jane?"

He wobbled. His legs buckled. Before he went down, he said, "My ex-wife."

2

He was going to throw up.

On his hands and knees in the deep grass, a tidal wave roaring in his head, Nathan contemplated a stand of lamb's-quarter. Cold sweat trickled down the side of his face. The ground in front of him slanted precariously.

The lamb's-quarter blurred, then his vision darkened from the outside in, like a solar eclipse.

He reminded himself to breathe—just on the off-chance that he wasn't. With that lungful of oxygen, he heaved a huge sigh, then put his forehead to the ground, to the cool, cool grass, and waited for the darkness to recede.

Jabbering.

Coming from somewhere in the distance, from somewhere behind him. Jabbering, jabbering.

A blue jay.

Scolding him. Chewing his ass out.

No. Not a blue jay, he decided through a mind-blurred fog. A *lark*.

He laughed a little at his wit, at his ability to find humor in the most dire of situations. The laughter helped to melt the tenseness in his shoulders, in the muscles behind his eyes, in his head.

The blackness receded. The queasiness in his stomach subsided.

He let out another sigh, this one of relief, and collapsed completely, his chest and thighs pressed to the hard ground, one bent arm supporting his forehead, and rested.

Just rested.

And while he rested, he tried not to think about Mary Jane.

About how she'd *looked*.

Puffy.

White.

Blue. Her mouth had been blue.

He groaned and rolled to his back, shading his face with a bent arm.

A hand touched his shoulder. Lightly. With concern.

He was thinking he wouldn't mind a little sympathy in his life when everything exploded.

His head went back; his spine arched. Beneath Lark's hand, Nathan Senatra's muscles turned rock-hard. She could feel the layering of sinew over sinew, of tendons wrapped over bone and under flesh.

A seizure?

She could only crouch next to him and stare in helpless, stupefied horror as he writhed before her, his body held in the throes of some unknown demon, his breath a painful rasp.

In hypnotic horror, Lark watched as he struggled to

lift his arm. Slowly, slowly, a clenched claw of a hand came up, bringing with it grass ripped out by the roots.

He let out a cry that was part agony, part aggression—and half-rolled, half-lunged at her.

The impact of his body sent her hurtling backward, knocking her to the ground. Her bottom made contact. That was followed by her back, her shoulders, then her head.

The next thing she was aware of was being crushed beneath the heavy weight of Nathan Senatra.

It was like sex. Sex with a total stranger.

He trembled a couple of times, then went limp, his weight pinning her to the ground, her breasts crushed beneath his chest, his breathing harsh and ragged and warm against her ear.

What in God's name?

Her mind was still reeling, her ears still ringing from the meeting of head and ground. She made a feeble attempt to shove him away.

No reaction.

She grabbed him by both shoulders, her hands unable to span his biceps, and gave him a shake.

No response.

She tried two fairly decent shoves.

He made a sound. A sort of muffled, mumbled reply. Then, ever so slowly, he lifted his head and chest, elbows braced on the ground, and looked down at her.

Somewhere in the last insane minutes, he'd lost his cap again. His dark hair was tousled and sweat-damp, his blue eyes a little out of focus. Then he grinned sheepishly and said, "Was it good for you?"

That's when she added screaming to her program.

Instantly, he rolled away, freeing her.

Within a second, she was on her feet, heart hammering,

legs trembling, hands clenched tightly at her sides. "*What's wrong with you?!*" she screamed, her voice shaking almost as much as the rest of her. "Are you *crazy?*"

It occurred to her that she may have stumbled upon the very answer to the entire conundrum.

Crazy.

He was crazy.

So simple. So to the point.

He'd told her to leave the farm. He hadn't wanted her snooping around. If you were hiding a body, would you want people snooping around?

He rolled to his knees, started to get up, seemed to think better of it, then sank back on his haunches, his faded flannel shirt falling across his thighs.

"What's wrong with *me?*" he asked.

She had to give him credit. He was a good actor. He could look affronted at the slightest instigation.

His breathing was still ragged. But now the uneven breathing was laced with anger. And disgust.

He may have killed once.

If so, he might kill again.

Could she outrun him? Could she get to her car and lock the door before he caught up with her?

Did he have a gun? If he had a gun, speed wouldn't matter. Not if he was a good shot. He could pick her off from a distance.

A knife? Did he have a knife?

Or had he strangled the poor woman?

Or simply held her under water until she'd died?

Had he—

His voice came slicing through her panic. It carried over the frantic pounding of her heart.

"You just sent seven thousand volts of electricity through me, that's what's wrong with me, city girl."

Her mind hadn't quite switched tracks.

Why had he killed her? What was the motive? Jealousy? Mone— "W-what?"

It took some effort, but he managed to shove himself to his feet. Once upright, he rolled his shoulders, then shook his arms as if he were shaking off water. Tested his neck muscles. Rubbed one arm, then the other. "You just shocked the hell out of me."

She struggled with the implausibility of his words. She slowly shook her head.

"See that wire there?"

She followed the direction of his pointing finger. Hidden in the tall grass was an innocuous-looking nylon string running parallel to the ground.

"That can't be. I didn't feel a thing." Not really true. Now that she thought about it, she recalled experiencing a slight tingling.

"While you were bent over touching me, some part of you, your shoulder, your ass, something, was touching the electric fence."

She stared blankly at him.

"I realize electricity is probably a little out of your field of expertise." His voice was full of scorn. It was obvious she was dealing with someone who held any experience in academia in supreme contempt.

"So here's a little electricity 101 for you. You touched me first, then you backed into the polywire. That makes me the ground. That makes me the one who gets fried."

She rolled that around in her head, then finally responded.

"Oh."

He was suckering her in. The whole thing was a cover-up, meant to throw her offtrack, to distract her. Make her forget about the dead body a mere thirty feet away.

Her doubt must have shown in her face—she'd always been transparent.

"If you don't believe me, I can demonstrate." He took a step in her direction. "Only this time you be the ground."

She wondered who was faster.

He was.

Before she could turn and run, he reached out and grabbed her by the arm.

"Ever been shocked by an electric fence? No? You don't feel it in your hands or feet, you feel it in your back, your chest, your shoulders. Kind of like being worked over with a two-by-four."

He pulled her toward the wire, a wire that had now taken on a most sinister quality.

She let out an undignified yelp, locked her knees, and planted the soles of her flimsy shoes firmly on the ground.

He released her and she almost fell over backward.

"Believe me?" he asked.

"Yes," she lied. She would have to do some research first. "But did you forget that the body of your ex-wife is just over there?" She motioned with her head, keeping her eyes on him, not daring to look in the direction of the pond, afraid she just might see something.

He passed a hand over his face and mumbled something about Mary Jane always showing up at the wrong time.

"We have to call the police," she reminded him.

"There's no hurry."

She was in a hurry. To get away.

"It's not like she's going anywhere."

"If you don't mind, I'll use your phone." Somebody had to do something.

"Don't have a phone."

"No phone?" Was he making it up? "Everybody has a phone."

"Not if they don't pay their bills."

She could believe that.

"The nearest phone is Rex's. It's a gas station in Elizabeth. You would have seen it if you came that way. I'll wait here while you go call."

That sounded like the best idea she'd heard yet. No way was she waiting with a corpse while he made the call.

She hurried through the pasture, away from the insanity, this time oblivious to the birds and the sun and the wildflowers.

Although the station was probably no more than two miles away, it seemed like ten. As Lark kept her eyes open for signs, she realized her hands were clamped to the steering wheel. She loosened her hold and started to shake.

Her idea had been to get away from the city, go to a nice little country town where people had gardens. Where they canned green beans and baked pies. A place where there were no car jackings, or muggings, or murders.

No rape.

Someplace safe.

Where people didn't lock their doors at night, and never took the keys out of their cars.

An hour into her pipe dream, and she'd stumbled across a possible homicide.

The gas station ended up being one of those locally owned places with a gravel-dust drive and no overhang to protect customers from the rain. Through a huge open door in the bay area, she could see a truck held up by a hydraulic lift.

She parked at the side of the cement-block building, where the rest room door stood ajar.

The air in the station smelled like stale cigarettes and grease. As soon as she closed the door behind her, conversation stopped. Three men at a card table looked up, stared a full four seconds, then looked back down, conversation picking up, but now carrying a preoccupied tone.

A teenager stood behind the counter.

"Can I use your phone?" she asked.

"If it's local." He slid the phone across the counter. His knuckles sported homemade tattoos that spelled LOVE and HATE. He probably didn't can green beans or bake pies.

She lifted the receiver, then realized she hadn't a clue who to call. She cleared her throat. "I, uh, wondered who I would call about a dead body."

Any conversation that had begun to roll came to a grinding halt. She chanced a peek over her shoulder.

Earlier, the men at the table had eyed her with suspicion and curiosity. Now their expressions were open, direct. And those expressions all said one thing: *What the hell?*

There was some dispute over exactly who she should contact. Suggestions ranged from the town marshall, who didn't carry a gun and whose main job was to keep the roads plowed in the winter, to the county sheriff. It was finally decided that the sheriff would be the best bet.

The kid behind the counter was too excited to find the number. One of the gentlemen from the card table, a man dressed in a green mesh pesticide cap and the bib overalls she'd been expecting, took the book, found the number, and dialed.

"Where's the body?" he asked while waiting for the police station to answer.

"Nathan Senatra's farm."

A couple of heartbeats of silence.

"The dreamer?"

Dreamer? Nathan Senatra? She quickly explained about the body of Nathan Senatra's ex-wife being found in the pond.

Someone at the other end must have answered. The man with the phone told them a body had been found, and where. "No, this isn't a joke. Send somebody out there right away." Then he hung up.

Everybody started talking at once.

"He finally done it."

"Always said he was nuts."

"Knew he'd go over the edge one day."

"Hell, he was over the edge before you were born."

"Wonder why he didn't kill her before this."

"Dreamer."

"Nature boy."

"Wait!"

They didn't hear her.

They kept up their chatter.

"Those unmowed ditches. Just an excuse for laziness."

"Nature habitats, he says."

"And that tree-hugger magazine. What the hell's it called? *Terra Firma?*"

A snort.

Wheezing laughter.

Lark decided she didn't like them very much. They may have been dressed for the part, but they didn't act it. They were more obnoxious than Nathan Senatra, and that was saying a lot.

She waved her arms to get their attention. "I didn't say it was murder!" She had to shout in order to be heard. "It could have been an accident."

"If it was Nathan Senatra's ex-wife, it was no accident."

Now that she'd finally gotten their attention, they were all looking at her, trying to figure out where she belonged in the equation. She certainly didn't want them to get the wrong idea, didn't want them to think she had anything to do with Nathan Senatra.

"I'm here about the cows," she stated.

"Huh?"

"Come again?"

"The cows. I'm here to conduct a study on the contentment of cows."

Four pairs of eyes stared at her. Then all four men burst out laughing. Right in her face. They laughed until they were breathless. They laughed until tears ran down their cheeks. They were still laughing as she marched out of the station, slamming the door behind her.

Nathan Senatra sat on the hilltop watching the driveway.

Lark Leopold had been gone a half hour when he finally spotted three clouds of dust moving in his direction between the unworked fields, like a cartoon.

The Roadrunner.

He'd always thought of the Roadrunner as kind of cruel. He'd always felt sorry for poor ol' Wile E.

The parade of vehicles pulled to a stop. Doors opened and slammed shut.

Shit.

Not a coroner or policeman in the bunch. Looked like the whole gas station crowd had come to take in the event.

Word gets around in a small town.

3

Officer Adam Trent was inching along Main Street in his squad car, checking parking meters, when he got the call from the dispatcher telling him a body had been found in his jurisdiction.

He liked checking meters. That and keeping the sidewalks safe from skateboarders were his favorite jobs.

Bodies he didn't like.

Especially female bodies. Hadn't the dispatcher said female?

He'd left Chicago because of dead bodies. He'd moved back home to Elizabeth in order to get away from big-city crime. Plus, with his parents both gone, his sister had needed him.

His first day on the job, and they'd put him in charge of crime-scene investigation. And parking meters. He preferred parking meters.

So far, the only crimes he'd had to investigate had been some break-ins and a few stolen cars.

He spotted an expired parking meter down the line and let out a sigh. Have to forget about that. Forget about stopping at the gas station for a can of pop and a candy bar. And he most likely wouldn't be going fishing later on.

Last year, a friend had offered him a job at a car dealership, but Adam couldn't see himself pushing cars. Some people got all buzzed up over engines and body style and tires. To him, a car was just a way to get somewhere. But now, with the news of the body, he wondered if he shouldn't have taken it. Now, instead of pushing Mazdas, he found himself swinging by the station in order to pick up an evidence kit he'd hoped he'd never have to see again.

At first, Adam didn't bother with getting in a big hurry. But when he got within two miles of the Senatra farm, traffic began to pick up. Another mile and it started to look like the road to Woodstock.

Adam flicked on the siren.

Cars reluctantly and belligerently moved to the side of the road to let him pass.

In Chicago, a dead body was no big deal. Nobody noticed. But in the country, where a neighbor's business often took precedence over your own, a stubbed toe was a major public event. A body would rank up there with a visit from the president. Or maybe a wrestler.

He cursed under his breath. It looked as if he was going to need more manpower to control the spectators.

He grabbed the radio. "Half the town is out here," he barked into the microphone. "We're going to need some volunteer police to control the traffic. I want the lane to Senatra's closed completely."

With the dispatcher's affirmative reply, he slid the mike back into place.

Nathan Senatra.

Adam smiled grimly to himself. After all these years, the guy was finally going to get what was coming to him.

Trent thought back to a time before he'd become a cop, before he'd graduated from high school, before he'd left Elizabeth for the big city. Back to a time when he'd beat the living crap out of Nathan Senatra.

He remembered going to his house, standing in the front yard, calling him out.

The sun was barely up. Senatra came to the door, all bleary-eyed and untidy. It probably wasn't a fair fight, but Adam hadn't been concerned with fair. He'd just wanted blood. And he'd gotten it.

Looking back, he could see that Senatra's heart really hadn't been in the fight. He'd only taken a few punches, then he'd quit altogether. Trent could still picture Senatra lying against the base of a tree, just taking it.

So Adam had left him there, with a bloody nose, bloody mouth, and swollen eye.

The satisfaction of feeling his fist making solid contact had been fleeting. But now . . . now was Adam's chance to really get back at Senatra for hurting his sister, for putting her in the nuthouse.

The lane to Senatra's farm was so congested with cars that Adam had to pull off the dirt and drive on the grassy area to get around some of the vehicles.

As he bounced along, his mood deteriorated more with each rotation of the tires. When he could go no further, he shut off the engine, grabbed the megaphone he usually used to clear skateboarders from the sidewalks, and got out of the car.

A circus. It had turned into a damn circus. He half expected to smell popcorn and hot dogs.

"Unless you're a witness, unless you have a formal statement to make, I want you out of here," he said into the megaphone. "*Now*. Otherwise you'll be arrested for tampering with evidence or obstruction of justice."

His threat had the desired results. People scattered. Within ten minutes, most of the cars were gone, along with the bystanders.

In another five minutes, the only people left were some policemen, the coroner, the suspect, and the body.

The coroner met him at the edge of the pasture.

Adam Trent and John Clark went way back. They'd known each other since vacation Bible School days. After a little small talk, they got down to business.

"I've pronounced the victim dead and called for an ambulance to transport the body," John said. "She was found submerged in the pond. When we arrived, the ex-husband had already pulled her out on the bank."

It was such a tranquil setting. A beautiful spring day. Sun warm on Adam's back. Birds singing.

"We were just waiting for you before we bagged her."

Adam fell into his role with reluctant ease. "Cause of death?"

"Looks like murder. Possibly strangulation. She has some bruises on her neck. I'll know more when I perform the autopsy."

"How long's she been there?"

"I'd guess it happened last night. She's still relatively fresh."

Side by side, the men walked in the direction of the pond. "What about the ex-husband?"

"Says he doesn't know anything other than the fact that she's dead and her body was in his pond."

The guy was guilty. Adam just had to put together enough evidence to prove it.

His mood didn't improve when he saw the crime scene. "Get these cattle out of here! This area should have been sealed!" Christ. The place was riddled with hoof prints. Any evidence they may have found was now driven deep into the mud. And no matter how guilty somebody looked, with no evidence, there was no case. It was that simple.

He caught two uniformed officers giving each other a look of exasperation. Adam knew they resented him for being so methodical. He knew that behind his back they made comments about how he thought he was a big shot because he'd worked in Chicago.

He didn't think he was a big shot. He just knew how easy it was to screw up evidence. He'd seen it done a million times. He'd done it himself.

They tried to shoo away the cattle from the crime area, but all they succeeded in doing was stirring them up. Within two minutes, they were running back and forth, bawling all over hell.

That's when Senatra decided to get off his butt and help. Within five minutes, the cattle were gone, moved out the gate to another pasture.

Adam approached the area where the body had been found, further dismayed to see that the cattle had done a thorough job of messing things up.

Regardless, Adam went about taking pictures, three rolls of film. Then he sketched out the crime scene, all with dates and times, collected the physical evidence, then canvassed a broader area for possible clues.

"Get a cast of this print." He pointed to an impression

of a boot's sole. It was most likely Senatra's, which wouldn't prove anything.

Then he went to get a written statement from Nathan Senatra.

The guy looked like hell. Adam almost felt sorry for him. Almost.

It had been several years since he'd seen him face-to-face. And Adam took careful note of his appearance.

Older. Leaner. Still had those blue eyes that seemed to look right through you. Still had that belligerent set to his mouth.

He was pale.

He was sweating from his run across the field after the cattle, but he wasn't out of breath.

He hadn't shaved in at least three days.

There were circles under his eyes, as if he hadn't slept much lately.

Adam found that most people, after killing someone, had trouble sleeping.

He opened the folder he'd tucked under his arm and pulled out a consent to search form. "We'll need to take a look in your house. The barn and outbuildings. Also your vehicle." He held out the form to Senatra. "You can either sign this or we'll get a warrant."

Senatra took the form.

Then Adam began to question him, wanting to know exactly what happened. A minute into Senatra's statement and Adam was putting a stop to everything.

"Wait a minute." He put up his hand, pen twined in his fingers. "Back up. Somebody *else* found the body? Somebody else was here?"

"Lark. Lark Leopold was her name."

Adam had never heard of her.

"She's here doing some dumb-ass study on cattle."

Adam looked around, but didn't see any other women in the area except for the uniformed police officer collecting samples. He'd reached the end of any patience he had. "Where the hell's the other witness?" he bellowed.

Heads came up. Faces turned his way, every one with a blank expression.

"For Christ's sake," he said with total exasperation. "Somebody go find her."

Lark had been laughed right out of town, that's what had happened. Laughed right out of town by a bunch of good ol' boys.

Still rattled, still shaking, she drove down the road, with no thought of where she was going. A warm wind gusted in the car's open window, bringing with it the scent of freshly turned earth and a crop yet to be planted.

She found herself behind a tractor, complete with the requisite slow-moving vehicle sign. Her speedometer read twenty miles an hour.

The tractor's left tire spanned the double yellow lines in the middle of the narrow county highway. The right tire rode the cement lip that must have been put there to fling unsuspecting travelers back on the road if they began to drift.

What now? Go home to Santa Barbara? Admit defeat?

She was an only child. Saying good-bye had been hard on her and hard on her elderly parents, especially with so many miles now separating them. There had been lots of tears on both sides. After being gone a total of three days, she could hardly go back. Could she?

It was tempting.

In the mornings, she and her mother would sit in the butterfly garden drinking flavored coffee and watching for hummingbirds. In the afternoons, they would pare apples and roll out pie dough. In the evenings, go for a stroll.

Not exciting, but peaceful.

And safe.

So very, very safe. And Lark liked safe. She *wanted* safe.

The tractor turned off the highway, the man in the cab giving her the friendly wave she'd expected from Nathan Senatra.

A sign read Leaving Metamora County.

Going home. To quiet, embroidered evenings and soft conversation.

Had she ever finished anything in her life?

She thought about her bottom dresser drawer, stuffed with unfinished projects. The needlepoint. The counted cross-stitch. The fabric painting.

Maybe taking a job in Iowa had been too big a step. She should have started small and worked up. Gotten something closer to home. Maybe a job at the Burger King a block from her parents' house.

No, she couldn't quit, not after such a short amount of time. Give it a few days, she told herself.

Reluctantly, Lark slowed to a crawl, then quickly executed a three-point turn. She'd barely straightened out when she met a police car. In her rearview mirror, she saw the red of his brake lights. Her heart jumped. She saw him slow, turn, then come after her, siren wailing.

Another first for her. She'd never before been stopped by a cop.

She pulled to the side of the road, gravel dust billowing in her window as she watched the approaching officer in her mirror.

He was young. And when he got to her open window, he turned out to be polite. Apparently not from the area.

She was nervously prepared to explain her U-turn when he asked, "You the one who found the body at the Senatra place?"

She nodded, heart pounding as she read the name on his badge. Officer Harris. The Harris poll, the rules from her memory enhancement class automatically falling into play. Richard Harris. He'd written a song about leaving a cake in the rain. What did it mean? Nothing, she'd always suspected. Only that LSD and lyrics didn't mix.

"We want you to come back to town and answer some questions."

Her heart beat even louder. Her palms began to sweat. "They don't think I had something to do with it, do they?"

"No, nothing like that," he said reassuringly. "You're a witness. We just need a statement from you. That's all."

"Of course." How stupid of her. She should have stayed around to talk to the police. She touched her forehead. "I'm just not thinking straight."

He smiled sympathetically. "That's understandable."

He was hardly more than a kid. He didn't scare her.

She wiped her sweating palms on the front of her skirt.

"Why don't you just follow me into town?"

She nodded, hoping the person who took her statement would be every bit as nice as Officer Harris.

One minute with Officer Adam Trent was all it took for Lark to decide she didn't like him.

He wasn't rude, he was intimidating. A big Rambo of a man, his uniform stretched across an expanse of chest. And dark. He was dark. His skin was dark. His hair was dark. His eyes were dark.

"Where are you staying?" he asked, leaning back in his chair while she sat across the desk from him, clutching her purse strap with both hands.

"I . . . I have reservations at River Oaks, the local bed and breakfast."

He smiled, or sort of smiled. White teeth flashed in his dark face.

"It's the only place in town," he said.

He had an accent she couldn't quite place. Not east coast. Not Midwest.

He asked her if she wanted anything to drink.

Water.

He got her a glass, put it down in front of her, and took his seat behind the desk. He waited until she'd taken a drink, then he began to question her.

How long had she known Nathan Senatra?

"I just met him." She tried to take another drink, but the glass rattled against her teeth and she had to put it down. All the while, Officer Trent silently observed her nervousness. She was acting like she had something to hide.

"What exactly are you doing here? What does your job involve?"

She took a deep breath and explained about the study, prepared for him to laugh like the others.

He didn't laugh. Instead, he nodded.

Thus encouraged, she went on to tell him just what had happened when she'd arrived at Nathan Senatra's that day. He appeared quite pleased when she got to the part about Nathan ordering her off his place.

When she was finished, Trent said, "I don't want you to put yourself in any danger, but I'd like for you to proceed with your study as planned. Keep your eyes and ears open. If you see or hear anything, no matter how small or insignificant it may seem, get in touch with me." He slid a business card across the desk. "Here's my office phone, home phone, and squad car."

"Do you think Nathan Senatra did it?"

An icy chill seemed to invade the room. Adam Trent showed some emotion for the first time. "I'm sure of it," he said slowly, his eyes hard, his mouth rigid.

He hates him, Lark realized with shock.

"A word of warning," he said. "Senatra's a ladies' man. He can sweet talk a woman into bed faster than you can say yes."

She'd had enough. Lark got to her feet, hitching her purse strap over one shoulder. "I've haven't been in Metamora County four hours, and I've been subjected to insult after insult, Mr. Trent. But I think I can honestly say that yours wins so far."

He drew back.

She'd surprised him. And for some reason, she had the feeling nobody had surprised him in a long time. Not that she cared.

The bed and breakfast was located right off the main street in downtown Elizabeth.

Already adjusting to friendly country ways, Lark wasn't surprised to find that the proprietor was every bit as charming as Nathan Senatra and Adam Trent. With a few unintelligible grunts, the woman who called herself Mrs. B showed Lark her room—a cubbyhole

Lark suspected had once been a closet. Her bed was actually a cot, and breakfast turned out to be access to the kitchen, with the guests supplying their own food and doing their own dishes.

A business could certainly get away with a lot of crap when there was no competition.

Lark was dragging her huge suitcase with the broken, useless wheels up the stairs one step at a time when the owner waylaid her on the landing. Where before Mrs. B's eyes had been flat and her expression almost hostile, she was now smiling. She actually took the case from Lark, telling her she'd put her in the wrong room.

Lark blinked and gave the woman a double take. Same dress. Same hair. Same face.

Twins. That would explain it. One twin had shown her upstairs the first time, now this one was carrying through with the welcome.

Mrs. B heaved Lark's suitcase onto a bed. A real honest-to-God bed. Beside it was a phone she could use to call her parents. Things were looking up.

"Did you really find Mary Jane Senatra's body?"

So that's what this was all about. The woman wasn't one of a matching set. She'd heard the news.

"Yes." Lark was unable to keep the impatience from her voice.

"Did Nate Senatra do it? I always said he was a strange one."

"I don't know." Lark had learned a few lessons in rudeness in the few hours she'd been in the area. She went to the door and waited for the woman to leave. "I really don't think I should be talking about this."

"Oh, everybody's talking about it. *Everybody.*"

When she realized Lark couldn't be seduced into gossip, Mrs. B left.

It appeared that the entire town was starved for entertainment. What an uncomfortable feeling knowing Lark was expected to supply it.

4

Five farms had signed up to be part of the contented cow study. Three of those five farms, including Nathan Senatra's, were in Metamora County. The other two were in the adjoining county of Saxon. One of the farms was a feedlot situation, the others were combinations of pasture and drylot. Nathan had the only herd that was completely pasture-fed, and that bothered Lark. Her job was to remain impartial, to simply take note of her observations, but she couldn't help but worry that his cattle had no shelter.

It turned out that the other farmers were much friendlier than Nathan. One young couple actually invited her inside for ice tea and cookies. But just as soon as she was sitting at the round oak table, they began to ply her with questions about the murder and about Nathan Senatra, a rabid lust in their eyes.

◦　◦　◦

Lark's days quickly fell into a pattern. She made her rounds, allowing an hour for each visit. That, combined with a stop for lunch and a total of two hours on the road, had her putting in an eight-hour day.

At first, she'd been nervous about running into Nathan. When Lark visited his cows, notebook and camera in hand, she would sometimes see him in the distance. On a tractor. In a truck. But he never stopped. He never even acted as if he saw her at all.

She began to relax. She quit looking over her shoulder. Quit jumping at the least sound. She even sometimes forgot that Nathan Senatra was a murder suspect.

The cows.

They absolutely enchanted her, something she hadn't expected. She'd always thought cows were cows. She'd probably never quite gotten over the Farmer Says version of farm animals. Simplistic. She'd thought cows were just animals that stood around, ate grass, mooed, and gave milk.

They were that and more.

She'd never seen animals that could express so many emotions with mere body language.

You could pretty much look into a dog's eyes and get a good idea of its mood. Dogs made faces. They growled. Lark had once known a dog that actually grinned.

With cows, it was all in the body. A cow's expression rarely changed, but little by little, Lark learned to read them.

There was the calm, take-a-munch-of-grass kind of thing. Then there was the bobbing, suspicious way they had of moving their heads. And in those early days, they did a lot of head-bobbing.

But then she became familiar to them. They would come and look her over, kind of say hello, then go on

about their business. And their business was eating.
Massive amounts. Their business was also lounging
around, digesting those massive amounts.

It didn't take her long to decide she liked cows. Liked
them very much.

Whenever Nathan saw her car come puttering up the
lane, he'd hightail it in the opposite direction. But on
the day he finished putting in crops, his curiosity got the
better of him. He parked the widow-maker in the shade of
the barn, got himself a drink at the hydrant, then headed
up the lane to see what Lark Leopold was up to.

It was dry as hell, he thought, his boots kicking up
clouds of fine dust that sought out every microscopic
indentation in jeans, socks, and workboots. They needed
rain. Bad. He'd hated planting those last twenty acres
when the ground was so dry, but he was pushing the sea-
son as it was. A hard rain now would pack the powdery
soil like cement. Nothing would come up. What they
needed was something gentle. Light. But nature could
be harsh. Unrelenting.

If he ended up in prison, none of it would matter anyway.

So far there was no new evidence in Mary Jane's
death. No new leads.

He was in big trouble.

Everybody thought he killed her. Hell, even his
grandmother thought he'd done it.

The day after Mary Jane's body was discovered, he'd
stopped by his grandmother's place to drop off the
green bananas she couldn't live without, hoping to tell
her an unembellished version of the story before she
heard it from someone else, but it was too late.

News, especially bad news, traveled fast in Metamora County.

He'd found his grandmother in her backyard, hanging up clothes. She was decked out in her rubber boots even though the grass was dry and it hadn't rained in almost two weeks. She had on one of her print dresses—she must have had a million of them. From the corner of her mouth dangled a filterless cigarette. Her eyes, behind thick spectacles, were squinted to avoid the smoke.

He scooped up the other end of the damp sheet, put the edges together, and held it to the line while she clipped it in place with wooden clothespins.

"Heard the bitch is dead," she mumbled around her cigarette.

Nathan made a little choking sound. After thirty-two years, she still had the moxie to surprise him.

"I told everybody you didn't do it. That my Nate wouldn't hurt a flea. But between the two of us—" She gave him a broad wink, took a final drag from her cigarette, dropped it at her feet, and put it out with one rubber-booted toe. "I wouldn't blame you if you had."

She was fishing. He could tell she was fishing, using the same bait she'd used when he was a kid. The I'm-on-your-side-no-matter-what technique. And through the years, he'd come to understand that she *was* on his side no matter what.

"I brought green bananas," he said, trying to change the subject.

"She always was trouble. Ants in her pants. And not just ants." She laughed at her joke. His grandmother had always liked to talk a little dirty.

That night after leaving his grandmother's, Nathan had taken it upon himself to do a little note-taking of his own. He'd put together a list of people who may have had a reason to kill Mary Jane.

It was long.

Mary Jane used people, and when she was finished, she threw them away.

It could have been any number of the men she'd dated. Like Denny Davis, the ex-marine. A nice enough guy, but he'd always reminded Nathan of the radio he used to have in the old 1086. Whenever the tractor hit a bump, the wires made contact and the radio would suddenly come on. But it never stayed on very long.

Davis and Mary Jane used to drink together, and do other things together. One day she up and dumped him. Davis tried to kill himself, failed, then found religion.

There was Hank Mitchell. He'd lived with Mary Jane for a time. He had a bulldozer, and Mary Jane used Hank to use the bulldozer to rip out every last tree on the place. When he'd finished desecrating the ground and planting some piss-poor crops, Mary Jane kicked him out. Poor old Hank. He'd figured on marrying Mary Jane and getting her land in the deal.

Hell, he'd even seen Adam Trent sniffing around her a time or two.

Then there was another angle altogether. Nathan wasn't all that popular. Some people saw his farming methods as a threat. It was just possible someone dumped Mary Jane's body in order to frame him, to make him look as crazy as some of his neighbors said he was.

And then there was the third possibility.

He may have killed her himself.

◦　◦　◦

Nathan couldn't stop the smile that tugged at one corner of his mouth when he spotted Lark. The day was warm and she was sitting in the grass wearing shorts and a sleeveless top along with hiking boots and white socks. Her hair caught the light, rippling like a wheat field. He'd didn't believe he'd ever seen hair like that. He found himself curious to know its texture, weight, smell.

Lark never saw or heard him coming. A shadow fell across her notebook and suddenly he was there, right beside her.

With a tired sigh, Nathan plopped down beside her in the shade of a maple tree, sprawling out, one long leg straight, the other bent, knee up. The knee of his jeans had a rip in it, horizontal, the edges frayed to soft white.

He took off his cap and hooked it over his knee. Then he tugged his fingers through his hair, pulling damp locks back from a forehead that was light in contrast to the rest of his face. He wore a faded blue T-shirt with ripped-out sleeves. She could see the muscles in his biceps, see his damp underarm when he lifted his hand to brush back his hair. He'd shaved recently, making the strong contours of his face easier to follow.

She recalled Adam Trent's words of warning, wondering if maybe she should take heed.

He pointed. "See those whorls on the cows' heads?"

She looked. In the middle of the nearest one's head, kind of between the eyes, was a swirl of hair, like a cowlick.

"They can be used to determine an animal's temperament."

"I'm not a total idiot," she said blandly. Next he'd be telling her he'd spotted the fictitious goosenflicker.

"It's true. The higher the whorl on the head, the more excitable the animal."

"Then what about that one?" She pointed. "It doesn't have a whorl at all." She had him now.

"Her? She's as tame as a puppy."

"I'm not falling for this," Lark informed him.

He shrugged. "Hey, they used to scoff about measuring a bull's testicles too."

"You don't say," she murmured, directing her eyes down at her notebook.

"Well, how about it?"

She could only hope he was taking the conversation in a new direction.

"Are my cows content?"

Wrong question.

"Look, Mr. Senatra—"

"Call me Nathan, or Nate—"

"I know you think this is all a hilarious joke, but I don't find animal rights amusing in the least. I'm monitoring five farms, and of those five farms, your cattle are the only ones that aren't inside at least part of the day!" So much for remaining impartial. "What about bad weather? Rain? Cold?"

He straightened, his body tense. "I think you've been watching too many *Hee-Haw* reruns. I'm not so ignorant that I need someone from Planet Utopia coming here to tell me how to take care of my livestock."

It had taken less than a minute for her to make him mad.

"Why don't you pencil-pushers go after the people who neglect their animals? The ones who don't feed them when it's cold, who don't supply them with shade and water when it's hot. The people who don't call the vet when they're sick."

He grabbed her tablet and pencil and slashed at it with an angry hand. "Cattle aren't people. That's what you can't seem to get through your heads." Slash, slash. The pencil moved across the lined paper. When he was done, he tossed the notebook back at her and jumped to his feet. "You're after the wrong man." With that, he strode away.

She got to her feet. "I'm not after anybody," she said, her voice trailing off. She looked down at the tablet in her hands. In big, dark, angry print, it read: LIVESTOCK 101. Under that was a drawing. A caricature.

Of a woman with long, wavy hair, bony knees, and huge workboots. She was offering a bite of hay to a cow's rear end.

"You jerk!" she shouted to Nathan's retreating back.

He kept walking.

The drawing was actually quite good. The cow was looking over its shoulder with an expression that said, What an idiot.

"My knees aren't that bony," Lark said to herself. "My feet aren't that big." She looked at her feet. "Are they?"

5

Nathan adjusted the water temperature at the kitchen sink until it was lukewarm. Then he filled the plastic bottle to the red, two-quart line, added the powdered milk replacer, shoved the rubber nipple down securely, and headed out the door just in time to see a police car rolling up his lane.

Shit.

He stood on the porch and watched as the white car pulled to a stop and Adam Trent stepped out into the early morning sunlight.

He adjusted a paraphernalia-laden belt that Nate had always assumed must have an annoying tendency to tug everything south.

Trent.

Why'd it have to be Trent? Somebody who'd had a grudge against him ever since their high school days, ever since Nathan had gone out with Trent's sister.

Talk about fatal attraction.

At the time, she'd seemed okay, at least *stable*. Sure, she'd been quiet and kind of nervous. Getting more than a sentence out of her had been a pain in the ass.

He'd never asked her out again, figuring it would come as a relief to her as well as to him. They hadn't exactly clicked.

Before he knew it, she was leaving notes in his locker and following him everywhere. She started telling people they were going together. She started telling people they were getting *married*.

Then she told people she was pregnant with his baby.

Up until that point, life for Nathan had been easy, no more than a summer vacation, or a dress rehearsal. Nancy Trent had taught him that everything you say, everything you do, means something.

He confronted Nancy, reminding her that they'd never had sex.

"You're lying," she'd screamed. "You know we did!"

She was convincing in her self-delusion. He almost believed her himself.

"Now I'm pregnant!" she said, sobbing. "And you're the father!"

He told her to go see a shrink. And then he walked away.

An hour later, she tried to kill herself.

She'd never really come back after that. Instead, she'd spent the last fifteen years in and out of mental institutions, leaving Nathan to wonder if he'd handled it differently that day, if he'd recognized that she had a serious problem and had tried to help her, things might have been different.

He'd never meant to hurt her.

Trent had hated him ever since he'd screwed up his sister's life. Who could blame him?

And that was why Nathan sure as hell didn't like knowing Trent was in charge of the murder investigation. Because Nathan knew there was nothing Trent would like better than to see him behind bars. Right now, the guy was probably regretting the fact that Iowa had no death penalty.

Trent approached through grass that hadn't yet had its first mowing of the year, the dew dampening the hem of his navy blue creased slacks, soaking his black regulation shoes.

Trent stopped and scanned the area. "See you have a widow-maker," he said, looking toward the barn where the end of Nathan's tractor could be seen. "Didn't know anybody had one of those anymore." His mundane comment proved that he was still small town, still had to shoot the breeze a little before getting to the real stuff. Nathan didn't think a comment about having no choice in the matter since his expired ex-wife had cleaned him out of everything would help his case. "I consider it a challenge," was what he settled for.

A memory came to him, something he'd forgotten all about until that very second. Trent's father had been killed in a tractor accident. If Nathan remembered right, Trent and his sister had witnessed it. Something like that could do weird things to a person's head.

"Talked to Beverly Barker down at Flo and Eddie's," Trent announced, getting to the reason for his visit.

Nathan's heart sank. He'd been waiting for this, wondering how long it would take before his excesses of that night became common knowledge.

"She says you were in the bar the night Mary Jane was murdered."

"That's right." No use denying it. Nathan just wished he knew where else he'd been.

"Says Mary Jane was there too."

Nathan shrugged, going for nonchalance. He put the nursing bottle down, crossed his arms, and leaned against the porch railing. "If you say so." All he could remember was sitting at the bar, drinking whiskey with beer chasers.

"Said you were pretty well lit by eight o'clock."

No shit.

He could remember Mary Jane coming in, but that was about it.

"Bev says you and Mary Jane got into an argument."

Was he bluffing?

"And that as soon as Mary Jane left, you followed her."

Was he trying to lead him into a trap? Or had he and Mary Jane argued? Had he really followed her? Good God. What if he had? Was he capable of murder? Was that why he didn't remember? A safety device? Selective amnesia?

"I have to go." He picked up the milk bottle, hoping that Trent didn't notice the way his hand shook. "I have work to do."

"Where did you go when you left the tavern?"

If Trent found out that he couldn't remember, he'd probably consider that enough grounds for arrest.

"So far, I haven't run into anyone who saw you afterward, but I've got about eight hundred people to go."

Maybe he'd better get a lawyer. Hell, maybe he should run, leave the country.

"Listen, Wyatt Earp, I didn't do it." He hoped his voice held a conviction he sure as hell didn't feel.

"I've also been by the courthouse. Guess what I found out?" Trent answered his own question. "That, since you have no children, everything you lost in the divorce settlement reverts back to you. The house. The land. The farm machinery."

He was screwed. Even if he hadn't done it, who would believe him? "Come on, Trent. Would I kill her, then dump her right behind my own house, practically in plain sight? Would I be that stupid?"

"Maybe you're just that smart."

Maybe so. Shit. Maybe so.

Nathan wasn't aware of any farewell on Trent's part, but he was sure it had come. It was the small town way. He just knew Trent was suddenly walking toward his car. Then he was driving away.

In Nathan's confused brain, years collided, time intertwined. Trent had come to Nathan's house fifteen years ago, the day his sister had tried to commit suicide, the news not having yet reached the Senatra farm. Nathan had stood there that morning, expecting to get chewed out for telling Nancy to see a shrink. Instead, the normally placid Trent had taken him by surprise and slugged him in the face, knocking him down, giving him a bloody nose. Furious at being caught off guard, Nathan had jumped to his feet, ready to go to it, ready to beat the hell out of the older boy when Trent, his face red with rage, spit out the reason for the attack, painting a vivid picture of his sister, lying in the bathtub, her wrists slit.

All the fight had drained out of Nathan.

That's how he felt now as he watched the police car move down the lane. Defeated. Ashamed. How had his life gotten so ugly? So messed up?

A beer mug so big it had to be held with two hands was the tip-off for Nathan. This probably wasn't real. He was dreaming. Sitting at Flo and Eddie's, smashing down one enormous drink after the other. Only the beer mug was like some huge water bucket he would have used for livestock.

A dream.

He was dreaming.

Mary Jane was there. Laughing. Buying drinks. She liked to spend money in a big way.

There was a guy with her. Nathan couldn't quite make out his face. He looked closer. Harder. Trent. It was Trent. That was strange.

Her voice came to him like tinkling glass, her words indecipherable. But the feelings they evoked were plain: Anger. Resentment. Disgust.

Tunnel vision took over. Everyone except for Mary Jane faded into the walls, including Trent. Vanished.

Nathan shouted at her. "You bitch!"

She left.

He followed.

Down a hallway that went on and on and on. A dead end. She turned. And for the first time since he'd known her, he saw fear in her eyes.

Finally.

And then she laughed.

He put his hands to her neck, to a throat he'd once kissed.

He squeezed.

Shadows moved in.

She was suddenly heavy in his arms. Limp. He lifted her, carried her, dropped her. She splashed into the water, sinking, sinking, watching him, watching him.

Nathan bolted upright, his eyes wide in the darkness, his body drenched in sweat. His heart hammered in his chest. His breathing was loud in the silence of the room.

He'd killed her. He'd killed Mary Jane.

An hour later, as rationality and daylight returned simultaneously, he began to doubt the dream. He was letting them all get to him. In a way, he was brainwashing himself.

6

Two days later, Lark stood in Nathan Senatra's pasture again, only this time it was cold instead of hot. Only this time it was raining.

Rain drummed against the plastic hood of the clear pocket raincoat she'd picked up at the hardware store in Elizabeth.

Her notebook was wet. The ink from her pen wouldn't flow across the damp pages. She gave up and jammed the dime-store pen into the metal coils of the spiral binding and contemplated leaving. The problem was, these were the very adverse weather conditions she'd been waiting for. Now she could observe how Nathan Senatra's cattle reacted to total elemental exposure—a phenomenon she'd have to make note of later.

Their reaction appeared to be no reaction. Not far away, they grazed, seemingly unaware of the ice cold rain.

She watched, amazed, admiring their stamina. Or was

it simply that they didn't know any better. Maybe ignorance *could* be bliss.

A tap on her shoulder had her jumping and letting out a low shriek.

Nathan Senatra stood there, coffee cup extended. Smiling. Or was he laughing? Most likely laughing like the rest of the county. Thinking how ridiculous she was, standing out in the rain.

While she felt quite unstylish in a raincoat with sleeves that were too short and armpits that were too binding, he somehow managed to look almost fashionable in a green poncho that fell to the top of brown knee boots. He hadn't gotten the hood situated quite right, and his dark hair was plastered to his forehead, his eyelashes clumped to spiked points.

Coffee. What a great idea. Why was he going out of his way to be nice all of a sudden? Perhaps he'd thought over their two previous encounters and had decided it would be to his advantage to make sure her conversations with the police weren't colored due to his rudeness.

Regardless of his motives, Lark welcomed the hot coffee. Her fingers were so numb she could hardly grasp the cup. "Th-thank you," she managed through frozen lips.

"I didn't know how you liked it so I didn't do anything to it."

"Bl-black is f-fine. Black is great."

Rainwater splashed in the cup, a cup she noticed was an advertisement for cattle wormer. Upon even closer inspection, she could see that the coffee was indeed very black. It even came with its own oil slick.

She took a tentative sip, almost choking on the acidic bitterness that coated her tongue.

"Little strong?" Without waiting for an answer, he added, "I made it yesterday." A pause for thought. "Or was it the day before?"

She tried another sip, partially out of politeness, partially because she couldn't fathom that anybody's coffee could be so terrible.

Wrong.

It could. It was.

Was it even coffee? Or something dredged from a river bottom?

She stood holding the cup, wondering what to do with it, hating to be rude, appreciating the thought, appreciating the warmth of the ceramic cup in her frozen hands, when he took it from her stiff fingers and tossed the contents on the ground. "Come on to the house and get out of this rain. I'll make a fresh cup."

Never hitchhike.

Never get into a car with a stranger.

Never use a cash machine in a secluded area.

Never wear stripes with plaids.

Never set foot inside a suspected murderer's house.

"N-no th-thanks."

"Your teeth are chattering."

She clamped them together.

"Your nose is red."

And numb.

"Your lips are blue."

"I like them that way."

He laughed.

She liked his laugh. It was open. Real.

Behind them, a flash lit up the sky. Half a second later, a crash shook the ground. She felt the reverberation in her chest. Then the sky opened up and rain began to come down in torrents.

She had no time to think. Nathan grabbed her hand, wet palms to wet palms, and pulled her after him.

They ran, the impact of their steps sending water shooting up around their feet. When they reached the safety of the porch, Nathan released her hand. It wasn't until then that she noticed how warm it had been.

She leaned against a white post and tried to catch her breath. Her tennis shoes were soaked, her feet squishing in her socks. Her jeans, below the knees, were dark from the rain.

Nathan pulled the poncho over his head. His green T-shirt clung to damp skin. She caught a glimpse of sun-tanned, hard-muscled stomach before his shirt fell back into place. He tossed the poncho over a porch swing, then kicked off his rubber boots, leaving him barefoot, leaving him looking extremely sexy.

"Take off your raincoat."

"No, I'd better go." She could just make out the blurred outline of her car, sitting forlornly in the middle of a growing puddle.

"Wait until the rain slacks off."

It only made sense.

Slowly, she unsnapped her raincoat, then lay it over the porch railing. Then she bent and struggled with the wet laces of her shoes, finally loosening them, pulling off her shoes, then socks. She squeezed out the water, dropping the socks on the porch next to her shoes.

The rain was coming down in torrents. It poured off one corner of the roof like water gushing from a fire hydrant.

She heard a pinging sound. Followed by another. Then another. Faster and faster.

Hail.

It was deafening.

She clung to a porch post and watched. "I've never seen a storm like this!" she shouted.

Just as quickly as it had come, the hail slowed until there was just the rain, until they could talk without shouting.

"You can't see the spot now, because of the rain," Nathan said, coming to stand beside her, "but there used to be a house there." He pointed. "A tornado came, picked up the house, and dropped it a half mile away."

"Like *The Wizard of Oz*."

"There was a guy in it. He didn't even get hurt." Then, "Come on inside. I'll make some fresh coffee."

He was right beside her. If she turned to look at him, their faces would be too close, so she kept her gaze directed out toward the driveway, the rain.

"I think the rain is slowing down."

The sky was still dark. The wind was picking up. But the safety of the porch seemed to create an intimate world. Too intimate. "I think I can make it to my car pretty soon."

She felt his eyes on her. She knew he was watching her. Knew if she turned she would be trapped by the blueness of his gaze.

Then she felt something on her back. He was touching her hair.

She stepped away. And now she did look up at him.

"You're afraid of me, aren't you?"

The directness of his question caught her off guard.

So what if she was afraid? Fear wasn't a bad thing. It had to do with survival.

"Maybe I'm just smart."

He took a step toward her, his blue eyes locked on hers. "You've been here, what, two weeks?"

"Y-yes."

"I suppose you've heard." It was a seductive whisper, words just for her.

"What?"

"That I'm crazy."

"You're deliberately trying to scare me. Why? Why did you bring me coffee only to turn around and get mean?"

"It's my nature. Hey, I'll admit, I'm curious about you. But you're also a threat. You could incriminate me. Then there's the cattle thing. You could shut me down. So effortlessly. With just a few words jotted on a piece of paper."

"I'm not that kind of person."

"How do I know that?"

"You don't."

"I guess you have to decide on what works for you."

"Distrust," she said. "That's what works for me."

He smiled a little and shrugged. Then, "What did you do before you came here? You said you worked for a research firm. What kind of research?"

"Not a firm, a private individual." If she told him she helped keep track of migratory bird patterns, then he'd know she worked for her father. And anyway, he didn't really care what she did. He was just sucking up. "You were right. It's basically a desk job." Something safe. Her own form of backpedaling. "You'd think it was boring."

"Sometimes I like boring things."

"Not this."

"Okay," he said, apparently taking the hint that her job was something she didn't want to talk about. "Tell me the truth. In your opinion, do I look like I could kill somebody?" There was suddenly a desperation in his eyes, as if he needed to know, as if he wasn't quite sure.

She'd once had an encounter with someone who had looked very nonthreatening. She'd been a college freshman and he'd followed her home to her apartment. He'd held a knife to her throat. And he had raped her. Over the years, the scars from the knife had faded, then finally disappeared altogether. But the emotional scars were as deep as ever.

Lark often despaired that she would never get past it, that she would never have a normal life.

"You can't go by a person's looks," she heard herself saying. "I think everyone is capable of murder, given the right circumstances."

She'd tried to fight back, she really had. She'd heard about people having super strength during an emergency, of being able to lift cars. It hadn't been there for her.

When he was finished with her, he left her for dead. And she would have died if her mother hadn't tried to call that evening only to discover that Lark's phone was out of order.

Later, Lark was told that the campus police found her. And that one of them had cried.

Nathan looked away, staring into the distance, his eyes focused on something in the past. Slowly he nodded his agreement. A chill moved across her, through her, and she wondered if she was looking at the face of a murderer.

Was she inviting violence into her life for a second time? Was it something she would never get away from?

He touched her again.

Like a deer trapped in headlights, she found she couldn't move away.

His thumb trailed down her neck, settling on the delicate skin of her throat. "Are you here to crucify me, Lark Leopold?"

He was so close she could feel his breath on the side of her face, so close she could see a tiny scar near his temple, so close she could see the marble pattern of his irises, could feel herself being pulled deep into the darkness of his pupils, of his mind. She didn't want to go that deep. Didn't want to know what went on in there.

Somehow she wrenched herself away, grabbed her shoes and wet socks and ran barefoot through the icy rain while the sound of his mocking laughter echoed behind her.

Her car was unlocked. Her keys inside.

Thank God. Thank God.

Heart hammering, she dove in, locking the door behind her. Shaking, she turned the ignition, put the car in gear, and drove away.

She wouldn't go back. She couldn't go back.

7

The pounding rain had packed the ground so that now, four days later, the surface of the fields Nathan had planted were like concrete. Without help, the seed sprouts would never be able to break through. Ironically enough, another rain would soften the soil, but there was no precipitation in the forecast.

Nathan had no choice but to get out the rotary hoe. It meant another pass over the fields. It meant more fuel, more time, more wear and tear on a tractor that was ready for the graveyard.

He got an early start.

The sun was barely a blush in the eastern sky when Nathan fed the bottle calf, filled the mineral feeders and creep feeders, checked to make sure all fifty-two head of cattle were well and accounted for, fueled up, dropped the two-pound metal pin through the eyes of the towbar, and headed out.

Nathan considered fieldwork just another way of saying

sensory overload. Like operating a jackhammer, a person could only take so much. Pretty soon, his taste buds were being tantalized by good ol' Iowa dirt, his ears by the deafening roar of the engine, his nose by the smell of burning diesel fuel and oil, and his entire body by the nonabsorbed impact of bone against bone.

It didn't take long for those senses to shut down, one at a time. It didn't take long for him to have an out-of-body experience where he just kind of Zenned it, giving his mind the freedom to go wherever the hell it pleased.

Used to be, Nathan liked to think. Not anymore. Lately he'd found himself rehashing the same stuff, getting nowhere. Mary Jane's murder. His being the prime suspect. And then there was Lark Leopold, showing up in the middle of everything, adding to his confusion.

Four days.

That's how long it had been since he'd seen her. She hadn't come around his place since the day of the big rain. So far, he hadn't made any points with her. In fact, he'd have to be way into the negative digits by now. He shouldn't have provoked her, but how was he to know she'd scare so easily. And anyway, she'd made him mad the way she'd treated him as if he were some escaped convict. Before he knew it, he'd found himself acting like one, just to get her back.

Stupid of him. What did he care what she thought? That kind of thing had never bothered him before. But for some reason, he'd wanted her to believe he hadn't done it. He'd wanted her on his side.

Which was doubly stupid, considering that he might be guilty.

Was she really as naive as she seemed? Or was it an act? *Nobody* was that naive, not unless she'd been raised in a convent.

He'd done the right thing, scaring her away. She shouldn't be hanging around somebody like him.

All the same, he wished she'd come back.

Throughout the morning, the temperature gradually rose. By noon, the thermometer attached to the above-ground diesel barrel read eighty-five. Without taking time to eat, Nathan refueled, got a drink, peeled off his shirt, dropped it on the ground, then returned to the field.

Pulling the rotary hoe didn't take as long as discing or planting. Two hours later he was halfway through the second field. His senses already saturated, it didn't take him as long to reach the hypnotic state. Soon his body was on autopilot—a nice place to be.

Maybe he fell asleep. Maybe his autopilot went bad. One second he was sitting there, hands on the wheel, his body bouncing up and down like some damn cartoon, when suddenly the tractor gave a tremendous lurch.

A new sensation.

This one was like being bucked from a horse. Or maybe shot from a cannon.

He was airborne, the ground hurtling toward him. He hit with jarring impact. First his shoulder. Then his side. Then his hip. Then his head.

Above him, the tractor roared, bearing down on him. The widow-maker, about to claim another victim.

He could feel the stoked heat from the engine, baking his face and bare chest.

Peripherally, he could see the crisscross pattern on the tractor's massive back tires bearing down on him.

Adrenaline rushed through his veins, alerting every nerve, vaulting across every synapse. A lifetime of information fed into his brain, all filed and registered within a fraction of a second.

Directly above his head—pedals.

Directly above his head—clutch.

With no time to translate a command into words, Nathan reached up, grabbed the metal clutch, and pulled it to the floor.

Gears disengaged.

The tractor stopped.

It took a minute for the adrenaline to slow. His brain waited for his thoughts to catch up.

Okay. Just hang on. Won't be donating any organs just yet.

There you go. Give yourself a minute.

Okay.

Don't let go of the clutch.

Now just get up. Don't let go of the clutch. Just get to your feet and turn off the tractor.

It was then that he realized his foot was caught, pinned by the back wheel, his body stretched like a rabbit on a spit.

Lark had been busy with her research. Ever since the day of the rain, many of the cattle she was monitoring had been sick. She watched as they were given shots, watched as pills were shoved down their throats. And every day she told herself she had to go back to Nathan's to see if his cattle were okay.

She usually saw him in the morning when she made her rounds, so she decided the thing to do would be to change her routine. Then hopefully she wouldn't see him at all.

◦   ◦   ◦

He was being punished. He'd killed Mary Jane and he was being punished.

His arms were being ripped from the sockets. They'd been stretched above his head so long he couldn't feel his fingers anymore. The only way he knew they were still wrapped around the clutch was because he was still alive.

God, the noise. The sound of the engine was deafening. And the smell. Diesel. Oil.

If he lived through this, he didn't know if he'd ever get that smell out of his sinuses. He'd never be able to smell anything again. No more alfalfa. No more rain.

Lark.

She'd smelled good. Like a flower. Or something green that grew wild in the woods—

He pulled in a startled breath. Hot liquid had dripped on his chest.

Fuel?

Water?

Battery acid?

God, please not battery acid.

He felt another drop. Hot. Was it acid? Acid would feel hot even if it wasn't. Could he feel it stinging? Burning? Eating a hole in his chest?

Oh God.

Just let go.

Let go!

It was unbelievable, but none of Nathan's cows appeared to be sick. They weren't coughing. There were none of the runny noses she'd seen at the other farms.

Content. They seemed very content. Except for one little calf that was making quite a scene.

Poor baby.

Nervous, hoping to get away before Nathan returne
she made a note of the calf, closed her tablet, took o
final scan of the pasture, and headed to where she'd le
her car unlocked and pointing in the right directio
ready for a quick getaway.

The muscles in his arms spasmed uncontrollably. H
coughed, tasting fuel, his throat raw from the fumes.

Earlier he'd tried to figure out how much fuel he ha
left to burn. Idling wouldn't use nearly as much as dra
ging a hoe back and forth across hilly ground. But sind
then he'd completely lost track of time so his calcul.
tions did him no good. He could have been hanging c
for hours . . . or minutes.

Had it only been minutes? That thought scared th
hell out of him. Scared him almost as much as whateve
was dripping on his chest, almost as much as the thre
of being crushed to death.

There were only two ways out. One was to hold th
clutch down until the tractor ran out of gas, somethir
that could take several hours. The other was to let g
and let the tractor run over him. The second choice w.
beginning to look better all the time.

Hadn't his life gone to hell anyway?

Lark was almost to the highway when a thought hit he
The calf. It had been bawling, not because it was lonel
as she'd first thought, but *because it was hungry*.

Some farmer she'd make.

She let the car coast to a stop.

The calf had never acted that way before. She shoul

know. She was the official observer. In fact, she'd often seen Nathan heading out to feed it.

So why was the calf so frantic today? Why hadn't Nathan fed it?

She turned around and headed back up the lane.

This time, when she got out of her car, she noticed things she'd been in too much of a hurry to notice before. A shirt, left carelessly on the ground. Nathan's small black truck in the shed. The tractor he'd been on the day she'd first met him, gone.

Even from such a distance, she could hear the calf, bawling, its little voice sometimes breaking completely as it cried itself hoarse.

Beyond the sound of the calf was something else.

An engine.

The steady *lub-lub* of an engine.

Here he was, just over the next hill, and he couldn't take time to stop and feed one baby calf.

She began walking in the direction of the engine, moving faster, getting angrier with each step. When she found Nathan Senatra, she planned to really chew him out.

8

In the far distance, a tractor stood silhouetted against a blood-red sky, unmoving, the engine running.

Something was wrong.

An irrational fear uncoiled in the pit of Lark's stomach. Where had that fear come from?

Nathan was having trouble with his tractor, or with the thing that was attached to the back of the tractor. People had trouble.

So why this novice bungee-jumper kind of feeling in her stomach?

She moved in the direction of the machine, gradually increasing her speed until she was practically running.

Slow down.

She was going to look like an idiot when she got there, out of breath and sweating. Nathan Senatra would straighten up from behind the tractor, a wrench or some other tool in his hand, and ask her why she'd decided to go for a jog in the middle of his field.

She slowed her pace, pulling in deep breaths. Then she stopped, rested her hands on her hips, and analyzed the situation.

Not a soul in sight.

Maybe he'd left the tractor running while he went to get something. A tool. His lunch. That was it. Tractors were probably hard to start, and once a person got one going, he didn't shut it off. Nathan had probably been in his house while Lark observed his cattle. He was probably feeding the bottle calf *this very second.*

Of course.

She was acting like her mother, worrying needlessly about things that would never happen.

She was about to turn around when something caught her eye. A color that didn't fit the hue of the rich soil or the faded green of the tractor.

Blue.

Seeing it there, in a place where it shouldn't be, made her think of the day she'd discovered the body.

But this time, instead of being in a pond, this blue was under the tractor.

"Nathan?"

No answer.

She tried again. "Nathan?"

Again, no reply. She ran, her feet stirring up the loose soil.

And then she saw him. Stretched out, naked to the waist. She could see the outline of his ribs, the indentation of his stomach, rising and falling in short, rapid breaths.

He was pinned under the tractor.

Oh God. No.

She dropped to her knees just feet from him. She could feel the heat from the laboring engine, smell the diesel, the oil.

"Nathan!"

It was a scream, a cry of panic and disbelief.

He didn't respond.

"Nathan!"

Her voice battled the deep rumble of the engine, the engine winning. He couldn't hear her.

She reached for him, her fingers lightly touching his forearm.

His arm muscles spasmed. Then his head came around. Slowly.

His eyes, his beautiful blue, blue eyes, when they finally found hers, were glazed and confused.

Her heart constricted.

"L-Lark?"

Her name was a question, spoken in bafflement, as if he couldn't quite grasp what he was seeing, as if she shouldn't be there.

"Nathan. Oh my God."

"G-get b-back." It took supreme effort for him to talk, for him to concentrate.

He squeezed his eyes shut. His breathing was labored. He was trembling all over.

What should she do? What should she do?

A million panic-stricken thoughts ran rampant through her head, none of them focused. Little by little, as she knelt there in the dirt, the heat from the tractor engine hitting her full in the face like a blast from a roaring furnace, the horror of the situation sank in.

Nathan was holding the clutch, his strength the only thing keeping the tractor from crushing him.

How long had he been there? How long had he waited for help? And more to the point, how much longer could he hang on?

"Nathan, tell me what to do." She couldn't keep the

panic from her voice. "Tell me what to do!" When he didn't respond, she put a hand to his thigh. The muscles beneath the soft denim were like stone.

He responded to her touch. His eyes came open again. And this time, she was relieved to see lucidity in those deep blue pools. She needed him. She couldn't do this alone.

He ran a tongue over dry lips. "Shut . . . it . . . off."

She looked up. Not far above her she spotted a small bronze key. Shut it off. Of course. So simple. So easy. Relieved that a turn of a key was something she could handle, she stood up. With a shaking hand, she reached out, wrapped her fingers around the key, paused, then turned it.

Nothing happened.

The engine was still running.

"Nathan!" She shouted down at him, keeping her eyes on the control panel, searching for something she may have missed. "I turned the key! Nothing happened!"

There was no answer from Nathan. She looked down.

Everything he had left was concentrated on the clutch. His body was covered with sweat. Tendons stood out on his neck. The muscles in his arms spasmed as he struggled to hang on.

Hurry.

She didn't know if it was her mind or his that screamed that single directive. Once more, her eyes scanned the control panel, searching, searching for something she may have missed, falling on a red knob labeled Throttle. It was pulled out. That had to be it, had to be what she needed.

Please God.

She pushed it in.

Nothing happened.

No! No!

But then, while a sob of despair choked her, the engine sputtered, coughed, and died.

Silence.

A blessed, ear-ringing silence.

She dropped to the ground. The tractor was off, but Nathan, although in no immediate danger, was still trapped.

Both of his hands still gripped the clutch pedal.

"Nathan, you can let go now."

He didn't respond. Instead, he kept his fingers locked around the pedal, hanging on as if his life depended on it, his muscles spasming out of control.

"Nathan—" She put a hand to his arm. "You can let go now!"

His head came around. His eyes sought hers, then dropped to her mouth, back to her eyes before returning to the clutch.

He can't hear me. He hasn't been able to hear a thing I've said.

Nathan saw her lips move, but could hear nothing but the hollow roar of the tractor engine. Roaring, roaring, just inches from his ear.

Had to hang on. Couldn't let go.

He felt her hand on his arm, feather-light against his screaming muscles. Couldn't let go. If he let go, she'd be crushed.

Then he felt her hand on his cheek, turning his face to hers so that they were eye to eye.

Have to hang on, he tried to tell her with his mind, his eyes.

She was saying something, but he couldn't hear her words above the roar of the engine.

Had to tell her. Had to make her understand. He pulled in a breath, the effort to speak almost too much. "Get—" He pulled in another breath. "A-way."

Instead of leaving, she continued to hold his face firmly in both of her hands, forcing him to look directly at her. Her lips moved. And this time, he read her words.

Off. It's off.

And then it came to him. The engine wasn't drowning out her voice. *He couldn't hear.*

Now, finally understanding that the tractor was no longer running, he tried to let go.

His fingers wouldn't open. They remained curled around the metal clutch like the claw of some bird. Hanging on for dear life.

She must have understood his dilemma, because suddenly he felt her small hands on his.

One by one, Lark worked his fingers loose until he fell to the ground, the impact creating a kind of rattling in his head, in the space between his ears.

He lay there for a long time, his chest rising and falling, his eyes closed, the feel of the soil beneath him a comfort.

Now that it was over, his entire body was limp, drained, useless. And yet it wasn't over. He was still trapped.

Lark was leaning over him, touching him, his arm, his face. Her lips moved, but he still couldn't hear anything but the roar of an engine that was no longer running. It wasn't until she got to her feet, until she turned and began to walk away that he understood what she'd been trying to tell him.

Before he could stop himself, he shouted. "Don't go!"

To his ears, his pathetic plea was a far-off cry, a weak echo down a long tunnel.

She heard him.

She came back.

He wanted to tell her about the diesel fuel, the battery acid. The foot he couldn't feel. But when she knelt back down beside him, all he could do was stare at her sweet angel face.

Evening sunlight slid down a strand of her beautiful hair, illuminating it.

She said something. And this time, he could hear the melody of her voice, like a gently moving brook. And even though he couldn't hear her words, he knew she was telling him she had to go and get help.

Don't go. Don't leave me.

He'd begged once, he couldn't beg again. Instead, he lifted a trembling hand. With numb fingertips, he touched the sunlight. He imagined its satiny texture beneath his work-rough skin. He carried the strand of hair to his face, his cheek. He inhaled. All he could smell was oil and exhaust fumes.

He felt a pain that had nothing to do with anything physical. It was an inexplicable sadness. An ache. A sorrow. A deep sense of loss.

It moved up his throat. And when he let it go, he felt a shudder in his chest, felt a sound he couldn't hear escape him.

He hoped to God she hadn't heard it.

But she had. He could tell by her expression. She was looking at him with soulful, shimmering eyes.

"Don't go."

One of his ears made a popping sound, like static on a radio.

Her lips moved. This time, the sound carried to his abused ears.

"I have to get help."

The reception wasn't great, but he could make out what she was saying.

"Lark, you can do it."

The implication of his words sank in; her eyes filled with panic. "I don't know anything about tractors."

"I'll . . . tell you . . . what to do."

She stared, nervously chewing her bottom lip.

She couldn't leave. He couldn't let her leave.

In the distance, coyotes howled.

Death calling.

He recognized the fragility of his mind. He was hanging by a thread. A very thin thread. *You're losing it, Senatra.* "I can't . . . stay . . . here . . . any longer."

The confession was torn from him out of desperation, a shameful thing, his voice a hoarse whisper, the words moving across a raw throat.

She must have at least partially understood the downward spiral into which he was being sucked because she suddenly pressed her lips together and nodded. She didn't think it was the thing to do. But she would help him.

He let his head drop to the ground in relief. While he lay there, he struggled to pull his thoughts together.

Whatever happened, he didn't want Lark to get hurt. That was the main thing, the thing he had to remember in all this. Lark couldn't get hurt.

And then he was telling her what she had to do. Slowly, carefully, one step at a time.

He could have given her a crash course in tractor driving, but if she put it in the wrong gear, then she would be responsible for killing him. He didn't want her to have that on her conscience. Or the tractor could get away from her. Tip over with her. No, it was better to keep her out of it as much as possible.

Before she could follow his instructions, he had to pull the clutch pedal down to the floor.

He couldn't raise his arms. His brain told them to move, but they wouldn't budge. Instead, they just stayed where they were, on either side of him.

Lark waited.

"Can't . . . lift my arms," he was finally forced to admit.

It was all she needed. "I'm getting help."

He ignored her. "Lift them for me."

"That's ridiculous."

"I can do it." Truthfully, he hadn't a clue. "Just get them up there."

"This is insane," she said, leaning over him. Using both hands, she grabbed one of his arms, lifted it above his head, placing his hand on the clutch.

Pain knifed up his shoulder. He swallowed a gasp.

"There's the clutch." Her fingers moved over his, folding them. "Can you feel it?"

His fingers locked around the metal.

She lifted his other arm into position, grumbling all the while, talking about getting some people to come, maybe dig him out.

Then the fingers of his right hand were wrapped around the clutch. Lying there, back in the same position he'd been in earlier, he felt a stab of panic. Maybe she was right. Maybe it would be better to wait.

This was the quickest way. And he couldn't wait. He was on the edge. A few more minutes trapped under the tractor and his mind would snap. Pretty soon, he'd be crying like a baby.

Lark got to her feet.

He took a few stabilizing breaths, then pulled the clutch down to the floor, disengaging the gears.

Above him, he heard Lark struggling to shift into reverse, heard metal hitting metal.

"It won't go in!"

The tractor was temperamental. Nobody knew that more than he. "Straight back," he said. "Straight back!"

"There! Okay. I got it!"

"Pull out the throttle, turn the key, and push the start button!"

"How can I be sure it's in reverse? What if I start it and it isn't?"

His arms were shaking viciously. He couldn't hold on much longer. "Don't give up on me now. Just do it!" If it wasn't in reverse, well . . . he'd be killed.

A calm came over him and suddenly the thought of dying didn't seem so bad. A good way to go, really. Out in the middle of his field. His one huge regret was that Lark would have to witness it.

"As soon as the engine turns over, get the hell away. As far as you can. Do you hear me?"

"Y-yes." Her voice was a trembling sob.

He heard the familiar sound of the engine sputtering to life, roaring, the throttle wide open.

He watched as she backed away, her eyes huge, a hand to her mouth.

He managed to give her a feeble smile, maybe his last. Then he released the clutch.

Gears connected. Metal slammed against metal. The back wheel lifted from his leg. Nathan rolled. Over and over, putting distance between himself and the tractor.

With no one driving it, the tractor was out of control, moving backward full-throttle toward a steep embankment.

Nathan watched as the small front wheels spun forty-five degrees. The rotary hoe jackknifed, catching the tractor. And then the widow-maker and hoe tumbled down the hillside, landing at the bottom with a huge crash of metal against metal.

9

Lark ran to where Nathan lay facedown in the dirt, dust settling around him. She fell to her knees beside him, adrenaline still pumping through her system, her entire body shaking.

"Nathan!"

He groaned and rolled to his back, eyes closed.

A fine layer of dust covered his hair, his face, contouring the muscles in his arms, his chest.

She'd saved his life. *She had saved him.*

She couldn't explain it, but in some strange way it was almost as if he belonged to her now.

And then his eyes came open, reflecting the light of the setting sun.

He stared at her. And looking into his eyes, she felt a kinship, a camaraderie. A bond.

But then, she began to pick up something strange. An uneasiness. Something close to panic was lurking in the depths of his dilated pupils.

"Nathan?"

He blinked, seemed to give himself a mental shake, and sat up.

Relieved, she concentrated on the moment, on his need for medical attention.

"I have to call for an ambulance. Oh. You don't have a phone. I'll have to go to the gas station." She tucked a foot under her, prepared to stand. "I'll hurry."

Wordlessly, he moved his leg, then his booted foot, testing for injuries. "Don't call anybody."

That was the first thing he said to her.

"What?"

"Don't call anybody."

"But your leg. Your foot . . ."

"It'll be okay."

"You had a tractor on it."

"My boots have steel toes. If I'd been on cement, it would be a different story, but the ground provided a cushion, kept any bones from being crushed. No, I'm okay. My foot's just a little numb, that's all."

It occurred to her that he was acting kind of strange, working a little too hard at convincing her he was okay.

As she watched, he pulled in a deep breath, started to lift his arm, apparently thought better of it, then let it drop against his leg. She was reaching for him when he abruptly said, "I want you to go back to the house. Fix a bottle for the orphan calf, feed him, then come back and get me with my truck."

She slowly got to her feet, letting her hand drop to her side. No thanks for saving his life. Nothing. Just do this, do that. If it weren't for the poor calf, she'd tell him just what she thought of him.

Without waiting for her to agree or disagree with his plans, he continued on, as if her services were understood.

He told her where to find the bottle, how to mix the powdered milk. Then he was thoughtful enough to add a little epilogue. "Get going. It'll be dark soon, and I don't want to have to find you tangled up in an electric fence."

What a jerk. It would serve him right if she just left him in the middle of the field.

"Is there anything else I can do for you while I'm at it?" she asked, her voice thick with sarcasm, sarcasm he apparently didn't pick up on.

"Pizza would be nice."

"Dream on, Jethro."

She gasped and put a hand to her mouth. She couldn't believe she'd said that.

He didn't even seem to notice. "Get outta here," he said, waving her away with one hand, appearing more bored and impatient than angry.

She hesitated. Maybe this was some kind of macho thing. Guys never could admit when they were in pain. Or when they needed a doctor. And he was acting a little funny. Even for him. Maybe he was going into shock. Maybe he really *did* need medical attention. And here she was, calling him names.

"I gotta take a whiz."

O-kay. "Maybe I'll just leave you out here. Maybe I won't come back. Maybe I have more important things to do."

"Like what?"

"Give myself a pedicure."

He reached for the top button of his jeans. "You'll come back."

"How do you know?"

Button undone, he went for the zipper. "I just know."

He was right. She searched her mind for a more

intimidating threat. "Just wait until you want to know every genus of the finch family."

He laughed at her. And then he unzipped his pants.

She spun around and stomped off across the field, her face hot, her teeth aching as she clamped her jaw tightly shut.

It took both of Lark's hands to hold the big bottle. She filled it with warm water from the kitchen tap, put in the milk replacer, and shoved on the rubber nipple.

Too bad she didn't have time to look around. His home was a place she'd been secretly curious about for some time. All she could do was store the stark images to retrieve and study at a later date. Then she headed out for the pasture, following the sound of the bawling calf.

The little guy was frantic, almost knocking Lark over in his haste to get the warm milk into his aching stomach. Within two minutes, the bottle was empty and he was searching for more, acting just as ravenous as he had before he'd started.

Feeling sorry for him, but knowing it wouldn't be good to feed him any more, she patted him on the head and told him good-bye. He couldn't have cared less. He made an awful noise, then butted her right between the legs. She let out a yelp and jumped back. "You ungrateful brat." It wasn't hard to figure out who'd taught him manners.

Nathan was just darn lucky she was such a nice person, she thought, striding angrily across the grass as she headed for the shed and Nathan's truck. Anybody else would have left him out there to rot. Or left him out there to crawl home. Now *that* was a nice mental picture.

She hadn't noticed the darkness, but suddenly it was there.

She found the truck and got in, shoving a bunch of clutter across the seat and out of her way. The floor was littered with what looked like sunflower seed hulls. They stuck to her dew-damp shoes. Ugh. He apparently spit the hulls out on the floor. How lovely.

It had been some time since she'd driven a stick shift, but she finally managed to get the truck backed out of the shed.

Find first gear. There you go.

Then she was heading up the dirt road that ran along the planted field, the headlight beams bobbing up and down as she maneuvered across the rough terrain in her journey to pick up the king.

She finally reached the area where she'd left him. She braked, dust drifting in the open window. Illuminated by the headlights was a pair of workboots. And a pair of socks that had once been white but were now an earth tone.

It figured.

There was no sign of Nathan Senatra anywhere.

She silently cursed him. Why hadn't he stayed where he was?

This was ridiculous. She'd only been gone a hour. Had he gotten impatient and tried to get home by himself?

She put the truck in neutral and jumped out. Hands on her hips, she surveyed the area, trying to see past the range of the headlights.

She could hear the loud whir of cicadas and the chirp of crickets. Up above was black, black night. On the ground, fog was beginning to gather. The spooky movie kind. The kind that wrapped around your ankles. The kind that moved and swirled.

In the distance, something howled and the hairs on her arms moved.

Where are you, Senatra?

Exasperated, yet beginning to worry in spite of herself, she got back in the truck, killed the headlights, turned off the ignition, and dug through the artifacts on the seat to pull out a flashlight she'd spotted earlier.

It was cheap. It was plastic.

She flicked the switch.

Low batteries.

With the excuse of a flashlight in hand, she got out of the truck and closed the door. Then she shouted Nathan's name.

Nothing.

Nothing but that creepy howling.

He's probably sitting at home laughing at me right now.

She tried again.

There!

Off to her left.

Splashing.

She followed the sound, moving through the darkness, her path lit by the weak yellow beam of the flashlight, the howling keeping her nerves on edge.

The night was warm, the field radiating the heat it had absorbed during the day. But every now and then, Lark would pass through a pocket of icy cold air. Someone had once told her those pockets were ghosts.

Her scalp tingled, and she decided a person's hair really could stand on end.

This was ridiculous. Nathan was probably in his house

right now, enjoying a hot soak in the tub while she stumbled around in the dark.

Suddenly the ground dipped and she almost lost her footing. She directed the beam down a sloped incline, exposing a valley with a stand of trees that ran the length of the field.

There!

A splash. Followed by another.

It was probably some animal down in a stream. An animal that might not like being disturbed.

"N-Nathan?"

Her voice would announce her presence. If it was an animal, it would run. Wouldn't it?

She followed the flashlight beam down the steep embankment. The soles of her shoes slid on the loose dirt and she kind of surfed down the hill until she ran smack into a huge tree. She pressed herself to the tree, a palm against its rough bark, and peered around—

Relief combined with supreme irritation was her first reaction. That was quickly followed by alarm.

Nathan stood thigh-deep in the water, jeans and all. Worse than that, she could hear his irregular breathing, sounding like someone who was terrified.

Someone who'd lost it. Someone who'd gone over the edge.

10

Oblivious to Lark's presence, Nathan sloshed handfuls of water on his chest, his arms, his face, as if trying to rid himself of something only he could see.

He'd tricked her.

His earlier cockiness had been nothing more than an act, a smoke screen.

"Nathan?"

She had no way of knowing if her voice would reach beyond his panic. No way of knowing if it would penetrate his mind. "Nathan, what are you doing?"

"B-battery acid. Gotta . . . get . . . it . . . off."

Her breath caught.

Gone was the smart aleck who'd barked directions at her.

Now she understood that something had happened to him out there under the tractor. He'd hung on as long as he could. And then, he'd snapped.

She moved away from the tree, moved all the way to

the water's edge. So as not to startle him, she directed the flashlight beam down. It skimmed across the ripples he was making. "Show me." She hoped to coax him back. "Let me see."

"Have . . . to . . . to get it off . . ."

Without another thought, Lark stepped into the water. Through the soles of her shoes, she could feel rocks, the size of someone's fist, making walking tricky. She moved toward him, the icy water rising up her legs.

The stream was narrow, no more than twenty feet across. It didn't take long for her to reach him. When she did, she put a hand to his arm. "Let me help," she said quietly. "Let me see if you've gotten it all off."

His head came up. She could see the glimmer of his eyes, knew he was looking at her.

"L-Lark?"

His question was hesitant, dazed, like someone awakening from a deep sleep. A nightmare.

When he was trapped under the tractor, he'd fingered her hair in a way that was so tender and so wistful, it had hurt. In that one crystalline moment, she would have done anything for him, believed anything he'd told her. In that moment, he'd been someone she could have loved.

This was the same man who had lifted her hair to his face, who had sobbed into it. With a flash of insight she understood why she'd been afraid of him. Now she understand that this was the man who could break her heart.

"Let me see."

She pulled at the hands he held splayed over his chest, his heart. She felt the stubborn rigidity of his muscles, the reluctance.

"Nathan . . ."

And finally his acquiescence.

With a sigh, he let go.

Beneath her fingertips, wet hair lay against solid muscle. She couldn't see or feel any sign of irritation. Combing her fingers through his chest hair, she tried not to think about how, under any other circumstances, such an action would be purely sensual. This was about reassurance. This was about bringing him back from wherever he'd gone.

"There's nothing there," she assured him with a firmness she prayed was convincing. "Nothing."

"Yeah?" His voice still trembled, yet at the same time, she thought she detected a hopeful note.

"Yeah."

He let out a shaky breath.

She was about to suggest they head for dry land when she felt his arms encircle her—and she realized the fingers of both her hands were still pressed to his chest.

It wasn't a situation that had been covered in her Women Alone class. Nothing had ever been said about standing in the middle of a stream, in the middle of the night, with a man she really didn't know.

He was shaking.

Against her breasts, her thighs, her stomach, she felt his body trembling.

"Let me touch you," he whispered. "I need to touch you."

Instead of pushing him away, she responded. One hand clung to the flashlight, her arm bent against his ribcage. Her other hand moved from his chest to the contours of his arm.

She felt his fingertips against her scalp, heard him whisper her name in a way that made her skin tingle.

"I couldn't let go," he whispered against her hair. "Why couldn't I just let go?"

It took her a moment to realize he was talking about the tractor. The meaning of his words sent a shock through her.

"It should have been so easy."

A tremor coursed through him. He was cold. Weak. They had to go, had to get dry.

"We can't stay here," she said softly.

She had no sooner spoken the words, when his legs buckled and he collapsed in the water, pulling her with him, the flashlight slipping from her fingers.

Darkness enveloped them. A shrill scream escaped her lips as water closed over her head.

Oh God. He's going to kill me, just like he killed her. Just like he killed Mary Jane.

She struggled.

Her head surfaced. She inhaled.

He held her by her arms, immobilizing her. She tried to wrench away, tried to pull free of his grip. But he wouldn't let go.

She went under again, swallowing water.

"Lark! Jesus Lark! What the hell are you doing? Stop it! You're going to drown! Stop it!"

She pounded at his arms, his chest, anything she could, struggling to free herself, struggling to get away.

"Lark! Lark!"

Finally the content of his words filtered into her panic-stricken mind.

She quit struggling.

Knee to knee, face to face, he held her by both arms while she coughed and gagged, her hands convulsing on his arms.

When she could finally breath without choking, he asked, "You okay?"

She nodded. "Yes." Her voice was a hoarse croak, her throat raw.

Then he did something every bit as strange as everything else that had happened up to that point.

He laughed.

Not just a little chuckle. This was an all-over laugh. A make-you-weak kind of laugh. A gasping, can't-get-my-breath kind of laugh.

Her first reaction was to take offense. Her spine straightened. Her mind struggled to formulate some scathing reply. But then she thought about how she'd thrashed around, about how she'd screamed and fought him—all in about two feet of water.

And she started to laugh.

What an idiot she was.

But then, as soon as she felt his hand on her throat, she quit laughing.

There was no way his touch could be mistaken for a threat. It was tender. Soft. The same touch he'd used on her hair.

And it stilled her breath. Stilled her heart. Stilled her every muscle.

Kneeling there in the water, in the blackness that was a night with no stars and no moon, she felt the callused tips of his fingers slide smoothly and lightly and erotically across the wet skin of her throat where her heartbeat was fluttering, fluttering. Every tingling nerve concentrated on that hand, those fingers, moving up her jaw, to the delicate spot just below her ear.

She felt the hot-cold wetness of his body as he leaned close. She felt the cool, damp, sweet warmth of his breath against her face.

She felt the softness and the chill and the heat of his

mouth against hers, a sensation that triggered a tight want deep inside her belly.

"*Lark.*"

Her name was a whisper, a caress, a tortured, surprised groan. As if he'd stumbled upon something he hadn't expected.

And then his lips moved over hers, all wet, and soft and wildly sensual.

These were feelings she'd never allowed herself to experience. These were feelings that were new and scary and wonderful all at the same time.

But then something happened to disrupt that feeling of exciting sexual euphoria.

A hand.

Full and bold on her breast.

Her nipple, burning through her wet shirt, erect against his palm.

For a second, terror kept her frozen.

Then she tore herself away, struggled to her feet. Gasping, she sloshed blindly through the water, reaching the bank, collapsing, getting up again.

Behind her, as her heart thundered frantically in her chest, as her throat closed in terror, came Nathan's sarcastic drawl.

"A simple *no* would have sufficed."

In the darkness, he couldn't see her terror, couldn't know the fear she had just experienced. Thank God. She didn't want him to know. She never wanted him to know. Ever.

Facing away from him, feet still in the water, she swallowed. Hard. "I . . . um. I'm sorry." Sorry. Why had she said that? Sorry she stopped him? "I'm s-sorry I lost your flashlight. It's so dark. But the truck isn't far away. Do you think you can make it? If you can't, I'll go for help. The flashlight. I dropped it. Maybe I can find it. I'll go find it."

Her voice rattled on, like some insane parrot. She wished she'd shut up. But then, if she stopped talking she might start crying.

She started crying anyway.

She needed to do something. She scrambled back into the middle of the stream, making a lot of noise, covering up her sobs. She collapsed to her knees and began searching the bed of the stream, her hands moving frantically over smooth stone after smooth stone.

And while she searched, she cried, tears running down her face, falling away into the dark water.

"Lark."

She jumped.

God. He was right behind her. She swallowed. She blinked. She willed her voice to come out normal. "It has to be around here somewhere." She sounded as perky as a girl scout. Well, maybe a hysterical girl scout.

Her hands moved over the rocks, testing the shapes, looking for something that didn't belong, half the time unaware of what she was looking for at all, too distraught to remember. Looking for the flashlight wasn't the point. Getting away from Nathan, *distracting* Nathan. That was the point.

"If . . . I don't find it, I'll . . . I'll get you a new one. But then, it shouldn't be left in the water. Batteries. Fish. Batteries aren't good for fish."

She was distantly aware of the role reversal going on. It was her turn to lose it.

"Lark."

She felt his hands on her shoulders. Lifting her to her feet, turning her around. "Forget the flashlight."

He wasn't laughing at her. She could tell by his voice. For once, she wished he'd been laughing. It he'd laughed, she could have gotten mad. And getting mad was so much better than crying.

No, he actually sounded kind. And that made her want to cry all over again.

"The batteries. The fish—"

"I'll come down in the daylight and look for it."

The voice of a parent speaking to a child. Calm. Soothing.

She forced herself to relax, forced herself to focus on the mundane. Mundane always brought her to her senses. "Yeah." She sniffled. She wiped at her nose with the back of her hand. "Silly of me."

He put his arm around her and steered her toward the bank. And his touch was comforting.

She struggled up the slick bank, then collapsed in the grass at the top.

Thank God for the darkness. She could feel the puffiness of her eyes, the redness of her nose.

Off in the distance came the howling she'd heard earlier.

Lark shivered.

"A coyote."

"What a sad sound."

He was silent a moment. "You ever feel sorry for Wile E. Coyote?"

"What?"

"Wile E. I know he was doing things he shouldn't have, but I figured it was instinct. I always felt sorry for the guy."

She knew what he was doing. Small talk. Fun talk. She needed it.

"I felt sorry for Sylvester. He was always getting into trouble for something he didn't do."

"Yeah." He heaved a heavy sigh. "Tweety Bird had a bit of a vicious streak."

Just as a mosquito bit her, she heard Nathan slap himself, a palm smacking flesh.

He grabbed her hand, pulling her to her feet. "Let's get the hell out of here."

11

He'd never seen a night so black, Nathan thought as they wandered across the field searching for his truck. Or a night so humid. It pressed down on him like a weight. It tripped him. Made him stagger.

His eyes were raw. His skin felt the way it did when he'd gone too long without sleep. Like it didn't fit anymore. Like it had shrunk.

He trudged on, his muscles screaming in protest, begging for him to stop.

The landscape of darkness was alien. What had once been familiar was unfamiliar. With each bone-weary, muscle-torturing step, he had the feeling he was plunging off the world into oblivion. The only connection he had to reality was the soft pressure of Lark's hand in his.

At the moment, that was enough.

They'd been walking aimlessly for the better part of fifteen minutes. Where the hell were they? They could be in Mexico by now for all he knew. Or South

America. Antarctica. He'd always wanted to go to Antarctica.

What he needed to do was lie down. Right now. In the middle of the field. Crash until the sun came up. It wasn't like they would freeze to death. It wasn't like a bear would happen by and eat them. It wasn't like they'd be sleeping in the middle of an interstate.

He was trying to link together enough words to verbalize his brilliant plan, when he felt a tug against his hand.

Lark had stopped.

"This way."

She tried to pull him in a new direction, but he'd had enough.

"Let's try this way," she insisted.

He couldn't go another step.

Sleep, sleep, sleep, until the sweet, sweet sun warmed his face.

Yeah, that was the ticket. That's what he needed to do.

His legs gave out and he crumpled to the ground.

The ground.

Soft as a pillow. Soft as clover.

"The earth is my bed, the sky my shelter," were the profound words he tried to mumble, but they slipped away and turned to gibberish before they left his mouth.

He didn't care.

His body thanked him for stopping. His muscles let out a collective sigh.

He felt Lark's hand slip from his. It was in his head to tell her not to let go, that they should stay together, but before he could finish the thought, he was asleep.

❖   ❖   ❖

Why had she acted like such an idiot? If she hadn't behaved so foolishly and hysterically back there, they'd still have a flashlight.

Would she ever be able to let a man touch her without flipping out? Probably not. No, and since she had no brothers or sisters, she wouldn't even have the luxury of being someone's goofy maiden aunt. No, she'd end up living alone. Neighborhood kids would dare each other to ring her doorbell and run. They would cross the street rather than get too close to her house, rather than walk on her weedy sidewalk.

Damp, clammy air brushed her bare arms, bringing her back to the situation at hand. Along with the damp air came the same smell that had stopped her short a while ago. A smell she associated with vehicles. A hot engine-oil-gas kind of smell.

She moved in the direction it seemed to be coming from, careful to keep Nathan directly behind her so she wouldn't lose track of him.

The truck found her. She smacked right into it, bumping her knee.

The truck! She'd found the truck!

She felt her way from the taillight, along the side panel, to the door handle. She pulled. Metal scraped metal, hinges creaking.

The dome light came on, casting a weak yellow glow. Was the *truck* battery bad? And then she had another thought. She reached past the steering wheel and clicked on the headlights.

All she could see was a solid bank of fog.

Cattle bawling.

No, a barn owl.

Owls were cool.

No, a ship's horn, sounding through a thick fog.

Or a thick head. Or a thick dream.

Someone shaking him. Shaking him. Shaking him.

Leave me alone, damn it.

"Nathan!"

A breathless voice. An excited voice. "I found the truck."

Lark. Lark of the incredibly soft hair. Of the incredibly soft lips. Lark, who'd saved his life. Lark, who had now apparently found his truck.

He wanted to sleep. To be left alone.

"It's not very far," she said. "Just twenty steps."

He felt a tug on his arm. He ignored it.

He really didn't give a shit if the truck was two feet away. He was comfortable. Put up the Do Not Disturb sign.

Women were always looking for something better. What was wrong with this spot?

A person didn't always have to sleep in a bed. Or sit in a chair. Or eat at a table. Those weren't *his* rules.

So what if he wanted to sleep outside? What did it hurt?

"Nathan."

She tugged at him again.

"Nathan, I found the truck."

He was lying on the ground, his face pressed to the dirt while she pulled his arm straight up. Didn't she know an arm wasn't meant to go that direction?

"Come on."

He had the feeling she wasn't going to give up. Pretty soon his arm would be out of the socket. He supposed he should get in the truck if his snoozing on the ground bothered her so much.

Problem was, he should never have stopped, should never have allowed himself even a few seconds of rest.

Rousing himself, getting to his feet, was very possibly the hardest thing he'd ever done. With Lark's misguided help, he managed to get his dogs under him. Once upright, he felt like a *World Book Encyclopedia* picture of the Cro-Magnon man, his arms hanging limply at his sides, his body hunched, feet bare.

With her arm around his waist, her body pressed to his side, they walked, one careful step at a time, until they reached the vehicle in question.

He didn't know what the fuss was all about. It was just a truck. It wasn't a time machine. Nothing would be different once they got inside.

If they got inside.

His body wasn't fully operational.

He tried to grasp the open passenger door to pull himself in. His muscles had gone on strike and his arms wouldn't work. He could kind of move them, he could even lift them, put them where he wanted them, but he couldn't make them do anything once they got there.

Getting into a four-wheel drive without using his arms was as challenging as a three-legged race. It certainly wasn't the most graceful thing he'd ever done.

He kind of rolled in, kind of wormed his way into the seat, with Lark shoving at him from behind, cheering him on.

He would have laughed if he'd had the strength.

Lark closed the door behind him, rounded the truck, and took her place behind the wheel. It wasn't until the engine had turned over and she'd switched on the headlights that he realized they had an even bigger problem than the darkness.

Fog.

No wonder his skin was so clammy. No wonder there was no sign of a moon or stars. The fog had obliterated everything.

Including the way out.

He groaned and slid down in the seat. "Why didn't you let me sleep?"

She turned on the wipers. "I couldn't leave you out there in the middle of nowhere."

The wipers had a spot in them where the rubber had worn through. That spot connected with the windshield, metal against glass, *click*, *click*, *click*, as the wipers beat fast and furious, trying to keep up with the heavy dew.

"You may as well shut off the engine. We'll never get anywhere in this." He crossed his arms over his chest, braced a knee against the dash, tilted his head against the headrest, and closed his burning eyes.

Instead of following his instructions, Lark put the truck in gear, turned it around, and began to drive slowly through the dense fog.

Nathan opened his eyes and dropped his bare feet to the floorboard, only then remembering that he'd left his boots behind.

Shit.

He didn't think he'd be able to find his way home through such a fog, and it was *his* land. Lark didn't have a prayer.

Turned out she must have had ESP or built-in radar or something, because she found the dirt road that ran along the north side of the field. Turning right, she followed it, moving slowly in the direction that should lead to his house.

Distance perception was skewed. What seemed like ten miles was more like ten yards. Nathan thought they were almost to the big maple that marked the northeast boundary of the field when he spotted a fence post he'd replaced last year. It gave him a bearing, telling him they'd hardly covered any ground at all.

Ten minutes later, they passed a familiar dip in the road, and before he knew it the headlights were outlining the corner post and the old oak that looked like a giant bonsai.

He pointed. "The road angles to the left here."

Lark sat perched on the edge of the seat, both hands glued to the wheel in the ten-and-two position, her nose inches from the windshield as she stared out into the headlight glare reflecting back at them.

As he looked at her sitting there, driving his truck with such focused intensity, he had a nice buddy feeling about her. He wanted to touch her, not necessarily in a sexual way, but a companionable way.

Who was he fooling? He also wanted to touch her in a sexual way. After he got some sleep.

Lark let out a little shriek, slammed on the brakes and killed the engine, all at the same time.

"Sorry," she muttered.

Nathan pulled his gaze away from Lark to squint through the streaked windshield. Directly in front of them was the iron base of a rusty windmill. Which could only mean one thing: They were in his yard, not far from his house. Another twenty feet and they would have driven through the porch.

Nathan opened the door and tumbled out, practically falling on his face when his muscles failed to respond. Lark followed more slowly, taking time to turn the ignition key and cut the headlights.

With the headlights off, the yard light took over. The elevated vapor glow, set high on a telephone pole, turned the world a gauzy gray.

Nathan rounded the truck and put one arm around Lark's shoulder, giving her a brotherly squeeze. "Nice going." Then he dropped his arm and headed for the porch, pausing when he realized she wasn't following.

She was looking in the direction of her car.

"There's no way you're driving back to town in this."

"I found my way here, didn't I?"

"Driving in the middle of a pasture is a little different from driving on the highway."

Regardless of his exhaustion, there was one last thing he had to do before allowing himself the luxury of sleep. He limped to her car, for the first time that night aware of a throbbing in his foot and ankle.

She must have figured out what he had in mind, because she was there right beside him. He opened the car door and pulled the keys from the ignition.

She tried to grab them. "Give those to me!" He lifted his arm high, holding the keys above her head.

Immediately, his arm started shaking. He lowered the keys. Before Lark could grab them, he tucked them deep in the front pocket of his damp, muddy jeans, a place he felt she wouldn't follow.

Lark glanced in the direction of his truck, where she'd left the keys in the ignition.

He let out a groan and rolled his eyes skyward. "All I wanna do is sleep. I won't be able to do that if I have to worry about you."

Lark thought about it, hating to admit that he was right. It would be extremely dangerous to try driving back to Elizabeth on a night like this. But to stay at Nathan's . . .

She could sleep in her car, but her clothes were wet and muddy. And a night spent sitting up didn't appeal to her in the least. Surely there was a couch she could use.

She turned to ask him.

He was gone.

She found him on the porch, lying face down on the metal glider, one arm dragging the floor, one tucked up beside him, his feet hanging over the arm of the swing.

Asleep.

How could somebody sleep like that? It looked terribly uncomfortable. He should have at least gotten out of his wet clothes. But she wasn't his mother. And she certainly wasn't going to wake him again.

Before stepping inside the house, she toed off her wet, muddy shoes. Then she opened the door and felt around on the wall, her fingers coming in contact with a switch. She flicked it. A single bare bulb screwed into a ceiling fixture cast a tepid, weak light.

The air of abandonment she remembered. The double porcelain sink, she remembered. Everything else was a new experience.

For a farmhouse, the building was small. The lower story consisted of a kitchen and an adjoining room. Nothing else. She assumed there was a bedroom upstairs, and hopefully a bathroom.

In the kitchen was an enamel gas stove that had to be about a hundred years old. It had six burners. One of them had most likely been used to concoct Nathan's delicious coffee.

The walls were of quaint, cream-colored wainscoting that, under normal conditions, Lark would have considered cozy. With the exception of the kitchen, the house seemed more a workshop than a place someone lived.

She stepped into the living room. There wasn't as much as a couch or chair. Instead, it contained things she recognized as woodworking tools. A jigsaw. A band saw. A lathe. From local gossip she'd learned that

Nathan had been forced out of his birth home, forced to move into this house after his divorce. Apparently he'd had no other place to put his things.

It seemed he was using the equipment to make potting flats. They were scattered around the room, along with several huge bags of sterile soil.

What in the world?

She was too tired and too physically miserable to take in any more. Feeling guilty about snooping through his house, but needing to use the rest room, she moved her tour upstairs.

The bathroom had hot and cold running water, plus a clawfooted tub and a toilet, the toilet being her main, immediate concern.

Finished in the bathroom, she stepped out into the hallway. Two doors, one closed, one open. The open door revealed an unmade double bed. She crossed to the closed door and turned the knob.

It was unlocked.

Slowly, she pushed it open.

Purple lights.

Windows covered with black paper.

What the. . . ?

The lights hung above makeshift tables of sawhorses and plywood. The makeshift tables held wall to wall wooden flats just like the ones she'd found downstairs. Except that these were full of potting soil. Except that these had grow lights above them. Except that they contained small, sprouting seedlings. Thumbtacked to the floral print wallpaper above them was a poster that said, BLOOM WHERE YOU'RE PLANTED. Under that was a huge marijuana leaf.

Good Lord.

Nathan Senatra was growing pot.

She'd had it. After tonight, she was washing her hands of him. After tonight, she would have nothing else to do with the man. That was if the police didn't pick this particular night to raid his place and name her an accomplice.

For now, she had no choice. She had to stay.

She went back to the first bedroom, the one with an actual bed. On the floor, she found a laundry basket full of clothes that were extremely wrinkled but appeared to be clean. From that, she dug out a flannel shirt and a pair of gray jogging pants that had been cut off to make long shorts.

Quickly, she stripped out of her wet clothes and replaced them with the wrinkled ones, marveling at how a simple thing like dry clothes could feel so wonderful.

Then she sat down on the edge of Nathan's bed. There were several rumpled pillows. Two homemade quilts. One in shades of red and blue, the other green and blue. The bed itself was soft, inviting.

He was asleep outside.

She couldn't leave until the fog lifted.

She would most likely wake up before he did.

She turned off the light and crawled into bed.

12

Sunlight pouring in the curtainless window woke her. At first she thought she was at the bed and breakfast in Elizabeth. Then she realized she was sleeping in Nathan Senatra's bed.

She let out a gasp and shot upright. Quickly, she scanned the room, spotting a digital clock on the dresser: 7:45.

This room was as sparse as the others. Nothing but a bed, the basket of clothes, and a pair of muddy sneakers. And of course the pile of her own muddy, wet clothes, which she'd been too tired to drape over the edge of the tub.

She felt a draft and realized her shirt—*his* shirt—had come unbuttoned during the night. She shot a nervous glance at the door. Still closed. She quickly buttoned the shirt. Then she gathered her wet clothes, rolling everything up in her jeans.

She couldn't put her wet, muddy things back on.

Surely Nathan wouldn't care if she wore his clothes back to town. After all, she'd saved his life. She'd give them back. And just so she wouldn't have to see him, she'd mail them to him.

Barefoot, she slid from the bed, opened the door, and hurried down the narrow wooden steps.

He was still outside on the porch. He was still asleep.

And he still had her keys.

Watching him, she put on her clammy, stiff canvas shoes. He was lying on his back, one leg bent, the other straight, his bare foot sticking out in the air. One of his arms lay over his chest, the other was bent so a hand supported his head. His mouth was slightly open. Not in a sloppy way, but actually an attractive, rather compelling way. His armpit hair was dark and sexy, surrounded by suntanned flesh and muscles. His nipples were perfect and round and dark—the shade of rich mahogany. His stomach was flat, hard-looking. His pants, now dry, were stretched across lean hips. And there, somewhere deep in the left front pocket of his jeans were her keys.

Last night she'd had a terrible time waking him. Last night he'd been a deep sleeper. Maybe he still was.

She stepped closer. And closer still. Until she was close enough to hear the evenness of his breathing. Until she was close enough to see the pores that harbored the dark stubble of his beard.

Just below his right eye was a small round scar. Chicken pox? If so, it was one of the nicest chicken pox scars she'd ever seen.

Her eyes tracked down, from his straight nose, past his full mouth, down his bare chest, to the copper button on the waistband of his jeans, and down . . .

Flustered, her gaze jumped to the right, to the front pocket of his jeans, then back to his face.

His eyes were open. And he was smiling sleepily up at her.

Good grief.

Her heart did a flip-flop.

The sensation was similar to the way she'd felt the first time she dove off the high dive at the public swimming pool. She'd stood there, perched on the end of the sandpaper surface of the board, the water a mile away.

Blue and deep.

Terror.

That's what she'd felt.

But also the promise of something wonderful.

The board was her friend. The water was her friend. But there was a vast amount of space in between that wasn't.

"K-keys," she stammered into that blueness. "I-I need my keys."

He grew pot in his bedroom.

He had bodies floating in his pond.

He was a marijuana-grower and possibly a murderer. She repeated it to herself, a chant to ward him off.

A marijuana-grower and possible murderer. Marijuana-grower and possible murderer.

"Don't go." He gave her a lazy smile.

He should have looked terrible. Anyone else would have. *She* would have. What was she talking about? She *did* look terrible. She'd caught a glimpse of herself in the bathroom mirror and it hadn't been pretty. But Nathan . . . well. Something else that was criminal. For a guy to look so good first thing in the morning.

He stretched a little. "Where did you sleep last night?"

There was no sense in lying. "Your bed."

He smiled again, seeming to like her answer. "And you're wearing my clothes."

"I hope you don't mind."

"I like it."

"I'll give them ba—"

"Are you wearing underwear?"

"What?"

"Underwear." He reached out and fingered the flannel of her shirt. His shirt. "I'll bet you're not."

His words made her doubly aware of her nakedness beneath the soft fabric of his clothes.

He took her hand. "Don't leave," he whispered, gently rubbing her fingers.

Then he began pulling her toward him.

He was half asleep. He was still exhausted. She could see it in the sexy smudges below his eyes. She could feel it in the tremors that ran through his arm.

"We could wake up together every morning," he said with a seductive promise.

This wasn't right, this game they were playing. She wanted to know a man, but not like this. Not this seductive, crazy, confused way. And not a man like Nathan. Please God, not a man like Nathan.

She'd often fantasized about someone. Someone without a face or name. He would bring her flowers. Not expensive roses. Maybe daisies. Or black-eyed Susans.

They would date. Go to a lot of movies. And maybe, after several months, they might kiss. And after a couple of years, they might . . .

And yet . . .

Maybe the thing to do was just dive in.

And yet . . .

She wasn't that kind of girl.

"I'm not sure that would be a good thing."

She tugged herself free of his hold, surprised to find that she felt a little disappointed that she hadn't given in and curled up next to him, thinking about how it would have felt to be held there, against his chest, feeling relieved that she didn't have to test herself.

He let out a resigned sigh. Then, moving very slowly, as if every muscle in his body hurt, he got to his feet.

She had to give him credit. He knew when to give up.

As she watched, he lifted his arm, then stopped, his hand poised to dig into the front pocket of his jeans.

"You're going to have to get the keys."

She put her hands on her hips and pressed her lips together. Apparently he *didn't* know when to give up.

"I'm not kidding, Lark. I can't move my fingers." He shook his head as if to give added emphasis to the seriousness of his problem. "After hanging onto that clutch for so long yesterday, my muscles are having a fit."

"You weren't having any trouble with them a minute ago," she said, recalling how he's rubbed her fingers so seductively.

"Other hand."

He had an answer for everything. She didn't know if she should believe him or not, but she had to reluctantly admit that his story made sense. Like any good lie.

"If you want the keys, you'll have to get them yourself."

It was a dare, plain and simple, regardless of whether or not he was lying. He wanted to see if she'd do it.

How ridiculous. She could reach into the pocket of someone's pants. She stepped closer. Then, after the briefest hesitation, she slid her hand into his pocket, working her fingers down at she went.

He watched her, an amused smile on his face.

"Deeper," he instructed. "You've got to go deeper."

He wasn't kidding. She was beginning to wonder just how deep the pocket went, when her fingers made contact with the jagged edge of a key, the metal warm from the heat of his body. She worked her fingers around them while Nathan continued to watch.

"I like you."

She stopped and looked up at him, into those blue, blue eyes. It would be a long dive. A very long dive.

"I'd like to kiss you."

He was beautiful.

She suddenly realized she didn't want to leave. When she thought of spending the rest of the day away from him, she felt empty inside.

But it was a dive she couldn't take.

She pulled the keys from of his pocket, spun around, and ran to her car.

"Lark."

She paused. She turned.

He stood on the porch, barefoot, bare-chested, hair a sleepy mess. "Thanks for saving my life." He smiled an ornery smile, flashing perfect white teeth. "You can sleep in my bed anytime."

She ducked in the car door. Within thirty flustered seconds, she was heading down the road. She'd gone a mile when she realized she'd left her bundle of clothes on the floor near his bed. Her jeans. Her T-shirt. Her bra. Panties. He would find them.

But there was no way she was going back.

13

Lark knew something was wrong before she ever reached Elizabeth.

People were looking at her.

In the cars she met on the road.

When she'd first arrived in Metamora County, she couldn't get used to the way people always waved, whether they knew you or not.

There were no waves today. Just stares.

She hadn't gotten enough sleep. That's what it was. She was just being paranoid.

Her first priority was a bath. She drove directly to River Oaks where she found Mrs. B industriously sweeping the gray front porch.

"Morning, Mrs. B," Lark said, climbing the enamel-coated steps.

Without lifting her gaze from the broom, Mrs. B said, "I was worried about you." Sweep, sweep. "You've never stayed out all night before." She stopped sweeping and looked up, a nightmare of a schoolmarm waiting for a tardy excuse.

Under the best of conditions, those being a good night's sleep, a shower, and a full belly, Lark would have had trouble reading the woman's expression. She appeared affronted, yet at the same time practically salivating in her need for her daily fix of gossip.

Lark stood with one foot poised on the top step. "I had to wait for the fog to lift."

"You could have called."

The woman was fishing, that was obvious.

"Mrs. B, I appreciate your concern, but I didn't realize I had to check in."

When Lark didn't fall into her trap, the woman just came out with it. "Nathan Senatra doesn't have a phone, does he?"

"What makes you think I was at Nathan's?"

"When you didn't come home last night, I called Officer Trent. He took a look around, saw your car, and called me back to let me know you were okay."

"I'm sure you were greatly relieved."

Mrs. B's pale eyes traveled over Lark's attire, taking in the flannel shirt, the cut-off jogging pants, the tangled hair.

Cripes. She hadn't imagined the sly glances, the knowing stares. Everybody in town thought she'd had sex with Nathan Senatra.

Word certainly *did* get around in a small town. And not the right word.

"If you'll excuse me." Lark brushed past her. "I really don't have time for this."

Lark heard a gasp of indignation and smiled grimly to herself. Her brusque dismissal of the older woman wouldn't gain her any points, but Lark refused to play games.

An hour later, showered and changed, Lark was thinking about food.

To eat meant either going to the grocery store, or stopping at the Feed Bucket, a local café where they hadn't yet gotten the word on cholesterol and fat. Lark figured her one meal there had set her heart back a year or two. It had taken days to get the smell of grease out of her hair.

Her other choice: Bob's Market. Both choices would mean having to leave her room. And *they* were out there.

This was ridiculous. Her run-in with Mrs. B didn't mean the entire town thought the same way. Did it?

She was about to leave when the phone rang.

Her parents.

"Hi honey!" A duet. Her mother was on one phone, her father, another. "How's everything going?"

"Going? Oh, well—" *I think I'm attracted to a guy who grows pot in his bedroom. Oh, and did I mention, he may also be a murderer?*

"Are you enjoying the peace and quiet there?"

The question came from her mother, a person who, even after Lark's rape, had somehow managed to retain the most idealistic, unrealistic view of the world a person could have. Lark didn't want to shatter it.

"She's probably bored out of her mind," came her father's dry comment. "Aren't you bored, honey?" He still hadn't accepted the fact that they wouldn't be working together that summer.

"Bored? Well, no, I wouldn't exactly say *bored*."

"Is it as humid there as your father claims?"

"Oh yes." The weather. A safe subject. "It's very humid."

"I told you it was humid."

Her father talking to her mother. Lark hoped they wouldn't start conducting a little conversation of their own.

"Your father watches the weather channel every day so he can see what it's like where you are. Last night they said there was a chance of heavy fog. Was it foggy?"

"It was foggy all right."

"I hope you didn't drive in it. You didn't, did you? That can be dangerous."

Before Lark could come up with some evasive kind of truth, her mother continued, "You won't believe this, but your father actually mentioned coming out to see you. Isn't that something? He hasn't gone on a trip in ten years. Remember when I tried to talk him into going to Arizona? He said he couldn't be away from his precious research that long."

"Have you seen many birds? How about a northern cardinal? Any American black ducks? Or a loggerhead shrike?"

"Sorry, Daddy. I haven't had much of a chance to look. I'll try this week. I promise."

"You've got the telephoto lens I gave you before you left, don't you?"

"Yes, Daddy. I've got it."

"Be sure to use high-speed film. You have to use high-speed film."

"I will."

Time for good-byes.

"I miss you."

"We miss you too, sweetheart."

After hanging up, Lark sat on the edge of the bed.

Now she was homesick. Thirty years old, and she was homesick.

Maybe she'd waited too long. Maybe it was too late to

change. Maybe she should just pack up her bags and head back to California. Her parents weren't getting any younger. She should be spending time with them.

That would be running. That would be giving up. She couldn't let the likes of Mrs. B drive her away.

She got to her feet, picked up her purse, and headed for the grocery store. Since it was only four blocks away, Lark walked. A brazen thing to do, considering the circumstances, but she wasn't going to hide. That would only make her look guilty.

A few minutes into her trip had her changing her mind. Hiding didn't seem like such a bad idea.

Was it her imagination, or were cars slowing down so the occupants could rubberneck? Yes, she decided, when a woman she met on the sidewalk actually stopped to stare.

She wanted to shout, to tell them all to take up a hobby.

Once she got to the store, things didn't improve. People shot her sidelong glances. A couple of sweet elderly women told her hello, then hung their heads in shame. Men smiled slyly at her. Everybody thinking the same thing. That last night she and Nathan Senatra had shared wild, passionate sex.

She found it impossible to concentrate. She finally gave up and hurried to the check-out counter.

"Paper or plastic?"

Brett Gillette. They'd met the first time she'd come to Bob's Market. He was about Nathan's age. Nice looking in a traditional sort of way, a nonthreatening, comfortable sort of way.

"Paper or plastic?"

He didn't seem as friendly as usual. She hated to think that he'd heard the lies.

He was still waiting.

Trees or chemicals. It was too tough. "You decide."

He shrugged and opened a plastic bag.

She paid. The cashier counted out her change.

Sex with Nathan Senatra. Sex with Nathan Senatra.

She turned. Brett stood there with two bags draped over his fingers.

Sex with Nathan Senatra. Sex with Nathan Senatra.

She tried to take the bags.

"I'll carry them for you."

"That's okay. I walked."

With his eyes directed down, somewhere in the vicinity of her shoes, he slid the bags from his fingers to hers. Then Lark was hurrying from the store, anxious to get back to her room, away from the prying eyes.

Lady Di had her utmost sympathy.

It was then she realized she was beginning to act as if she were guilty. No wonder accused suspects sometimes confessed to crimes they never committed.

She'd only left Nathan's house a little over two hours ago, and *she* was beginning to believe that she and Nathan had done it.

Back in the kitchen of River Oaks, she unpacked her groceries and was surprised at what she found.

She didn't know she liked anchovies. And she was sure she'd never eat such a large can of prunes.

Three days later, she ran into Nathan at the most unlikely place. The grocery store, where she'd returned to get the things she'd hadn't picked up earlier.

Their carts almost collided when she rounded the corner of aisle three.

"Lark. Hey." He actually looked glad to see her. Good actor.

"Hey."

Lucky for her, she wasn't the only one involved in the contented farm animal study. There were a hundred observers like herself scattered all over the country; the final results didn't hinge on a single individual.

She hadn't been to Nathan's place in days. Not since that night. Her record book, which should have held notes on the Senatra cattle, was a collection of blank pages.

She gripped the plastic handle of the cart with both hands and leaned into it like someone ready to shove a wheelbarrow full of dirt uphill. He didn't take the hint.

"I have something of yours."

People were looking at them. It was like being lead center stage.

He was going to announce to everyone in the store that he was in possession of her bra and panties.

"Keep them."

His eyebrows lifted in exaggerated surprise. "Your notes?"

"What?"

"I found some pages of your notes." He leaned closer, his face all concern. "What did you think I was going to say?"

"I don't know," she lied, spotting Brett Gillette at the end of the aisle, stocking the shelf, trying to keep one eye on his work, one on them.

"They're at the house. Pick 'em up next time you come by. You are coming by again, aren't you?"

"I'm not sure."

"The cows miss you."

"Ha ha."

"They've been asking about you."

"Is that right?" What kind of game was he playing?

"Yeah."

"Oh really."

"Really."

She was poised to go, when he added the kicker.

"We could make it true."

"Get out of my way so I can get by." She grabbed a loaf of French bread from a display and threw it in her cart. It landed next to a box of tampons.

She looked up to find Nathan contemplating the contents of her cart.

"Feeling a little grumpy and out of sorts, are we?"

"Move your cart."

"I guess I should be glad it's not a home pregnancy test kit, right?"

"Go to hell."

Lark had to ram her cart into his in order to get past him. But she managed. Then she was moving quickly down the aisle, one wheel of her cart clicking loudly, announcing her location to everyone in the store.

Sex with Nathan Senatra.

Sex with Nathan Senatra.

This time Brett carried her groceries to the car, putting them in the backseat. "I wanted to ask you something," he said, closing the door and turning to face her.

He looked so earnest, so serious. *Here it comes*, she thought. He'd going to ask me if the rumors are true.

"Would you like to go out sometime? To a movie maybe?" Behind him, she spotted Nathan coming out of the grocery store.

"Why, yes. I'd like that. I'd like that very much."

Exactly five days later, Brett came to pick her up in an old blue Chevy he'd completely restored. And he brought her flowers. No man had ever given her flowers before. It made her want to cry.

They ended up going to the drive-in, to a movie Lark had seen on videotape a few years earlier. The sound was bad, the picture was bad, but the novelty of a drive-in theater made up for it.

It was like going back in time.

Lark loved it.

Brett. He was a surprise. A total surprise. She found out he'd gone to the University of Illinois. That he had a graduate degree in psychology.

"You were expecting some hillbilly, weren't you?" he asked as he drove her back to River Oaks.

"No." But she hadn't expected so much. "Of course not."

"I work at the grocery store because I want to. Because over the years I've come to realize I don't want complications in my life."

As they headed up the street toward the bed and breakfast, Lark spotted a familiar black truck parked at River Oaks. Standing in front of it, under the canopy of a huge oak tree, hip resting against the grill of his truck, arms crossed over his chest, booted feet crossed at the ankles, was Nathan Senatra.

Brett parked facing him on the wrong side of the street. He cut the lights and engine, then he and Lark got out.

Behind Nathan, on the truck hood, was a paper bag, top rolled neatly down. "Since you haven't been to my place," he announced casually, reaching behind him for the bag, "I thought I'd drop these things off while I was in town."

Lark grabbed it from him before he could open it and dangle her bra and panties for Brett to see.

Brett had followed her from the car, and now he stood just behind her left shoulder.

Awkward was the word of the moment.

"Do you two know each other?"

Nate stuck his hands in the front pockets of his jeans and gave a nod. "Hello, Brett."

"Nathan."

Lark sensed an undercurrent. They knew each other all right. And didn't like each other. Wasn't this nice? A perfect end to a perfect evening.

All three stood there in silence. It was Nathan's move. In a place where people played by the rules, Nathan should be the one to leave, to extend his apologies for interrupting their evening. He either didn't know about the rules, or he didn't care.

"We've been to a movie." Lark waved her hand in the direction of the drive-in.

Nathan nodded. And Lark suddenly had the feeling her announcement wasn't telling him anything he didn't already know.

More silence.

Was this some kind of standoff?

"I've got an early day tomorrow," Brett said, the only gentleman among them. Gentleman enough to relieve the awkwardness of the situation. "I'd better be going."

With Nathan present, there would be no plans made for another evening out.

Brett backed toward his car. "You two apparently have something to talk about."

"No— Brett," came Lark's immediate protest. "Wait."

He opened the car door. "Catch you later." He got in his car and was pulling away when Lark called after him.

"I had a nice time." She waved. A hand shot out the open window.

After his taillights disappeared around the corner, Nathan said, "You shouldn't go out with him."

"What?" Who was he to chase away her date? Tell her who she could and couldn't see?

"Just what I said. You shouldn't go out with that guy."

"And why not?"

He shrugged with a feigned lack of interest. "He's weird."

She let out a sputtering, indignant laugh. "He's smart."

"Why would somebody with a master's degree in psychology be sacking groceries at Bob's Market?"

"He wants a simple life. There's nothing wrong with that. As people get older, they sometimes realize that what they thought they wanted wasn't what they wanted at all. And the things they threw away become the things they need."

He wasn't listening. He was staring at something.

"What's that?" He pointed.

She looked down. In her hand was the straggly bouquet of flowers Brett had given her. "Flowers," she said in a dreamy voice.

"Flowers." He let out a snort of disgust. "Looks like a handful of damn weeds to me."

"They're daisies." She stroked the white petals against the side of her face. "I thought it was very sweet of him."

"Sweet, my ass."

He was in a very bad mood. And it was quickly rubbing off on her. "I've been thinking," she told him. "About whether or not I should tell the police about you."

That perked him right up. He straightened away from the truck. "What do you mean?"

"About your gardening project."

He looked blankly at her.

The man was a consummate actor. "In case Mrs B was listening at her bedroom window, Lark leaned close and whispered, "The *marijuana*. I know about the pot you're growing upstairs. So if you ask me, you're the one I shouldn't be hanging around with."

She'd surprised him. Maybe even shocked him.

Good. He deserved it. After ruining her date, after disparaging poor Brett.

"You're right," he said, seeming to measure his words carefully. "You shouldn't be hanging around with me. I don't know what I was thinking."

Suddenly it was all wrong. Why, she'd hurt his feelings. She'd never meant to hurt his feelings. What had she said that hadn't been the truth? What had she done?

Before she could stop him, he was in his truck, backing up, making a U-turn, his tires squealing in his haste to get away.

Mrs. B met her at the front door. "I want you to know we can't have all these men hanging around here," she said, clutching the collar of her pink polyester housecoat close to her throat. "I've always run a clean place. People will talk."

Lark was in no mood to deal with Mrs. B. "And you won't mind getting the ball rolling."

The older woman's eyes narrowed. "I don't start gossip, I just pass it on."

In her room, Lark sat on the edge of the bed and opened the paper bag Nathan had brought. Inside were her clothes. Only now, instead of being muddy and wet, they were clean. Along with her clothes were the notes she'd lost. Plus several new pages, written in a man's sharp, strong handwriting, bringing her records up to date.

Along with the new records were sketches. Funny ones. Charming ones. Of cows. And calves.

Damp night air blew in the open truck window, whipping Nathan's hair about his head. What the hell had he been thinking, going to her place like that?

Over the past couple of weeks, Brett had been on and off Nathan's suspect list. Off more than on, but still, the guy just kind of gave Nathan the creeps. He tried to tell himself it was just because he was weird. But Nathan had to be honest. There was a good chance he was hung up over the fact that Brett had gotten the education Nathan had never had.

He should have gone to college. He'd planned to, but when his parents had died one right after the other, there had been no time. Almost overnight, his life went from easy to complicated. Suddenly there weren't enough hours in the day to get all of the farmwork done, let alone go to school. One day he'd been a kid, the next, an adult. And the easy part never came back.

It shouldn't have mattered, but Nathan didn't want Lark to know that he'd never even finished high school.

Then, when his grandmother, who was gossip central, had told him Lark was going on a date with the Big Brain, well, he just kind of lost it.

What was new?

14

Lark tried to get back on track. The very next morning she headed out early. She put in a full day, making her rounds, taking extensive notes. The cattle in feedlots were still sick, but improving.

She went to Nathan's last. After observing his cattle for a couple of hours, she left without seeing him, feeling even more depressed.

At River Oaks, she pulled to the curb and cut the engine. There was something in the yard.

Something that looked suspiciously like her suitcase.

And her clothes, strewn around in the grass!

Lark jumped from the car, slammed the door and charged up the front porch to the door.

Locked.

She pounded.

In the downstairs window, a curtain moved.

"Mrs. B!" *Pound, pound.* "Mrs. B!" She'd keep yelling

until the woman came to the door, until she gave her some explanation.

The inner door finally opened and Mrs. B appeared, glaring defiantly at Lark through the locked screen.

"What is the meaning of this!" Lark waved an irate hand in the direction of her violated belongings.

Mrs. B's chin lifted slightly. "I can't have a tart like you staying in my bed and breakfast."

"A *what*?" Lark choked.

This was insane. She hadn't been with a man since, since . . . well, she'd *never* been with a man. Not the way it should be.

Frustration and anger and confusion had been building in her for the past several days. Now, she'd finally found release. "You are such a shallow busybody." She jabbed her finger in the direction of Mrs. B's chest. "When you've run out of things to talk about, you make them up!"

Mrs. B straightened as much as she could. "Ever since you showed up here, waving that blond hair around, wearing those shorts and hiking boots . . ." She shook her head. "Men in the street. Arguing. Tires squealing. I can't have you coming to your room in the middle of the night. Or not coming to your room at all."

"You want to know about the other night?" A voice deep inside Lark's head said she was going to regret this, but she didn't care. She was on a roll. "Well, I'll tell you about the other night. I had sex! You want to know what else? It was great! Wonderful!" She backed up a few steps and shouted. "Sex! Sex! Sex! On the porch, on the ground, on the kitchen table. That's why I came here. I'm not really doing a study on farm animals. That's my cover. No, I came here to have sex!"

She charged down the steps, gathered up her loose clothes and suitcase, and stormed to the car. After tossing everything in the trunk, she charged back to the house, to the door where Mrs. B still stood, a smug expression on her face.

She would have enough gossip to last her days, weeks, months.

"I want my groceries."

Mrs. B stared.

"My groceries," Lark repeated.

The woman left, then returned with a wrinkled paper bag. She unlocked the screen, quickly shoved the bag at Lark, then closed the screen and locked it.

Supporting the bag with one arm, Lark poked through the contents. "Just making sure everything's here." She pulled out the can of prunes and set it down on the porch. "You need these a lot more than I do. You've been looking a little constipated lately."

And then she left.

At first, it was like being released from prison. But then, the aftermath of her adrenaline rush wore off and the euphoria faded.

Depression set in.

Every day for the last several days she'd thought she'd hit rock bottom. But everyday she tumbled a little lower, a little deeper.

She found herself pulling into a semicircular drive of a roadside park, complete with picnic table, water hydrant, and outhouse.

A home away from home.

She turned off the engine and stared blankly at the wall of trees in front of her.

Where was she going to go? She'd stayed on at River Oaks, not because she'd been so taken with the quaint Mrs. B, but because there was no other place to stay for fifty miles.

Not wanting to give up was one thing, but Lark had to admit she'd probably reached the point where it would be foolish to keep hanging on. What was she doing in Elizabeth, Iowa, anyway? She didn't belong there.

She'd come, hoping to fix her own problems, to find an answer, to get past what had happened to her all those years ago. Instead, she'd stumbled into a world of real people with their own real problems. A world where she didn't belong.

It was getting dark and she was exhausted. Lately, she'd had trouble sleeping. Now she found she was too tired to drive. Too tired to think.

She put her seat down, crossed her arms, and closed her eyes. If only she could sleep. With some sleep, maybe she could figure out what to do.

Knocking.

Right next to her head.

Lark came awake with a start.

She was in her car, at the rest area, and someone was knocking on her window.

She opened her eyes—and was blinded by a flashlight beam. The beam shifted slightly. Beyond the starburst image burned into her retina, she saw a police badge. A blue uniform.

Officer Trent.

Two run-ins with him were enough for Lark. He scared her.

She pushed the window button. Nothing happened. The key. Had to turn the key.

She turned it.

The window whined down.

"Miss Leopold?"

"Hello officer." She struggled to get her bearings, her brain sluggish. Apparently she'd been asleep, and for quite some time according to her aching joints and stiff neck.

"Everything okay?"

"I fell asleep." She rubbed a spot between her eyebrows—the center of a dull pain.

"This rest area isn't zoned for camping."

She dropped her hand and looked up at him, exasperated. "I'm not exactly *camping.*"

"And I shouldn't need to tell you it's not a good idea to stay the night out here. Especially after a woman's been murdered."

He was talking as if there was a serial killer on the loose. She'd thought Mary Jane's murder had been an act of passion, committed by a close acquaintance. Lark had never considered herself, or any other woman in the county, in danger.

"I'll leave. I'm leaving. Right now."

"Oh, and Miss Leopold. I want to let you know that Mrs. Barrington has filed a complaint against you."

"A complaint? For what?"

"Verbal abuse."

"You mean threats?"

"That's what she says. Now just to keep everybody happy, I told her I'd give you a trespass warning. You're not to step foot on her place, or have any contact with her. Understand?"

"I'm the one who's been victimized! I'm the one who got thrown out and left with no place to stay! The woman is a vicious gossip. She slandered me!"

He smiled a little at that. It was the first inkling that he had any sense of humor at all. "Around here, it's not called slander, it's called conversation. I know how hard

she can be to get along with. I'm just trying to calm h
down so she doesn't do anything stupid, like trying
take you to court or something."

"I'm the one who could take *her* to court. For defam
tion of character."

"If you need a place to stay, I could probably fi
somebody with an extra room."

"No thanks." She didn't want any help from him. A
she certainly didn't want him keeping tabs on her.

"We've already gotten a statement from you. If there
nothing else you can think of that we need to know, the
you're free to leave the county."

Was he kicking her out of town? The idea was lud
crous.

"Just be sure and give us an address where we c
reach you when this Senatra case goes to trial."

Trial. She'd never really thought it would come
that. She didn't know what she thought would happe
Maybe that someone would come forward and confes
Or the killer would be found. And that killer wouldn't l
Nathan.

"You have enough evidence to arrest Nathan?"

"Not yet, but it's only a matter of time."

He seemed so sure of himself.

"I'm going to go back to my car and wait until you'
on the road," he told her.

Lark thought about how she wouldn't mind using th
outhouse. Wouldn't mind brushing her teeth at th
hydrant. Instead, she turned the ignition key.

Nothing happened.

She tried again.

Nothing. The starter didn't even make a sound.

"Pop the hood and I'll take a look."

She pulled the release lever.

Officer Trent lifted the hood and looked inside while Lark got out and joined him.

"Here's your problem." He pointed. "Spark plug wires are gone."

"Gone?"

He straightened, hands on hips, his expression serious. "Somebody crawled under your car and pulled them out while you were asleep. You're hard to wake up," he added, as if that explained everything.

"Why would somebody do such a thing?" Her knees went weak. Her mouth was so dry she could hardly swallow. She could have been murdered. She could have been raped.

"To keep you from leaving town."

"I don't understand."

"Here's another idea." He looked her directly in the eye. "Maybe you did it yourself."

"What? Why would I sabotage my own car?"

"A foreign job like this will be hard to get parts for. Nobody in this area will have the wires in stock. Gives you a good reason to stick around." He concluded his theory. "I've heard you and Senatra are getting pretty tight. Women do strange things when they're hot for a guy."

Hot for a guy? From the very beginning, Trent had treated her in the most disrespectful way, trying to diminish her as best he could. She was tired. She was cranky. And she'd had enough of his attitude. "You pig."

He blinked, his expression quickly changing from cocky to one of disbelief. A muscle in his cheek twitched.

Her heart pounded as she stared right back at him. "You heard me right. I called you a pig. And I don't mean pig like policeman pig. I mean pig as in less than a man."

As she defiantly watched him, his face took on its typical blankness. "I could have you arrested for that." He slammed the hood shut. "But I won't. Get in the squad car. I'll give you a lift to town, to the garage so you can make arrangements for a tow truck."

He turned and walked toward his car, expecting her to follow.

She didn't want to follow. Even if she hadn't just called him a pig, she wouldn't have wanted to follow. "Why don't you have them come and pick me up."

"I'm not leaving you here by yourself."

"It's not dark anymore."

During the last few minutes, the sun had come up, its rays reflecting brightly off the dew, off the siren and spotlight of Trent's patrol car.

"Doesn't matter. Whoever did this might be back. Or he could be nearby."

At least he seemed satisfied that she hadn't done it. She glanced around. The area was surrounded by a thick wall of trees. A person could easily hide there. But she didn't want to go with him. She didn't want to get in a car with him.

Which was ridiculous.

She got her purse and keys, locked her doors, and followed him to the patrol car.

Maybe *he* did it, she thought. Maybe he pulled the wires, and now he was going to take her someplace to kill her and dump her body. Otherwise, he could just call the garage from his squad car.

He's a policeman.

So? Policemen went crazy just like everybody else.

Behind them came the sound of a car. It slowed. It pulled off the road, gravel crunching under tires.

Lark turned and saw a baby blue Chevy.

The door opened and out tumbled Brett Gillette.

"Lark! I've been looking for you all night." He was out of breath, his normally neat hair a mess, his button-down shirt, wrinkled. "I heard you got kicked out of River Oaks."

What a relief. She was surprised and touched that he'd been worried about her. Now she wouldn't have to get in the car with Trent. Brett could give her a ride.

Brett filled her in on Trent's history on the way to town. "He used to work with the Chicago police, but he flipped out. Just went totally bonkers one day. Was in the nuthouse for a while. Then therapy."

"I knew there was something strange about him," Lark said. "What set him off? Do you know?"

"I guess he's always been a little nutty. When he was about ten, he saw his father get killed. A tractor accident. The tractor tipped over on him, crushed him."

"How awful." She thought about Nathan, about how the same thing had almost happened to him.

"Yeah, it was pretty bad."

"Were you living around here then?"

"Yeah, but I was little. I don't remember much of it."

"And then what happened? In Chicago?"

"He was assigned to some serial killer case. Where the victims were women. Guess it was pretty grisly. I don't know if it's true or not, but supposedly his girlfriend ended up being one of the victims."

Trent was always so emotionless, so removed. No wonder. "So he came back here, thinking he'd get away from it all."

"Yeah. Strange, isn't it? How it followed him?"

Lark shivered, thankful she hadn't gotten in the car

with Trent. Glad Brett had happened along when he did.

Trent had been right about the garage having to order new wires.

"Could take several days," she was told. In the meantime, she made arrangements for a tow truck to pick up her car.

"Looks like you're stuck here awhile," Brett said as they left the garage and headed for his shiny blue Chevy.

"I don't know what I'm going to do." She rubbed her aching head. "Where I'm going to stay."

"How about my place?"

She looked up, startled.

"I'll sleep on the couch."

"Oh, I don't know." It was tempting. There Brett was, standing in front of her with all the earnest sincerity of a preacher.

"I don't care what people say, if that's what you're worried about."

A quick burst from a police siren had them both looking up.

Trent.

He pulled to a stop a few feet away, dust flying. Then he got out of his car, holding some sort of long rubber tubing with capped ends.

Brett looked surprised. "Where'd you find those?"

"Those" were apparently spark plug wires.

"Got 'em off a car in the junkyard," he told them. Then, to Lark, "Get in. I can have your car running in less than fifteen minutes."

He seemed awfully anxious to get her alone. Or maybe he was just anxious to get her on her way. Whatever his reason, she didn't relish the thought of riding in a car with him.

Once again, Brett came to her rescue. "I can do it," he said, putting out his hand for the rubber-covered wires.

Trent shrugged. "Have at it."

A half hour later Lark's car was back in running order.

"You saved my life," she told Brett as they stood next to her car.

"Hardly."

"Close to it."

"I meant what I said about staying at my place. The offer still stands."

"That's sweet, but I think I'm going to head home."

"To California?"

"This just hasn't worked out the way I thought it would."

"Life rarely does. Maybe you just haven't given it a chance."

He was watching her with a scrutiny that made her feel slightly uncomfortable. Had he heard the stories about her? Had his offer of a place to stay been purely self-motivated?

But then he smiled, the shy, self-conscious smile she was now familiar with.

This place was making her paranoid.

She got in the car, shut the door, and put down the window. "Thanks," she said. "For everything."

"Sure. If you change your mind, my offer's still open. Anytime."

She left him standing in the rest area.

◦ ◦ ◦

Before leaving the area completely, she had some bird-watching to do. And she had some clothes to drop off.

The bird-watching didn't go well. Not well at all. In fact, it went so poorly that it was dark by the time she got to Nathan's house. From a distance, as she rolled up the lane, it looked cozy, the paned windows casting a warm glow.

Near the windmill stood the tractor that had almost killed him. It was battered and bent. She hoped it couldn't be fixed. She hoped he would never drive it again.

Her car had barely stopped when she jumped out and hurried to the porch, afraid that if she moved any slower she would chicken out.

She rapped her knuckles against the kitchen door, stepped back and waited.

When he answered, he looked sexy and tired and surprised to see her. He must have just gotten out of the tub. His hair was wet, his T-shirt damp in spots, his feet bare.

She handed him a bag with his clothes in it. "You've won. Trent won. Mrs. B won. I'm leaving."

Exhaustion washed over her. Did she have the strength to go through with this?

She shouldn't have come.

"Before I go, I wanted to ask you one thing."

He stood there, waiting, wordless for a change. She sensed that he was thinking, that he was running her news around in his head.

"Did you do it? Did you kill her?"

Still he said nothing.

What had she expected?

For him to say no.

And if he told her he didn't do it, would she believe him?

She'd try. So very, very hard.

He ran a hand through his wet hair, pushing a fallen strand back from his forehead. "Did I do it?" He gave a pained laugh and cast his gaze skyward, then back at her. His answer, when it came, was one she hadn't expected.

"I wish to hell I knew."

It wasn't what she'd wanted to hear. It didn't help her at all. Not at all. "You don't *know?*"

"The night Mary Jane died, I was drunk. I don't remember anything. Not anything at all."

Oh God. This was something. Really something. His news hurt. Why should it hurt?

She laughed, and the sound was full of self-mockery. She couldn't face him anymore, so she turned away. She walked down the steps, her feet feeling like lead.

She'd come to Iowa, hoping to unload some of her baggage, some of the weight that had been bearing down on her soul for so many years. Instead, she'd picked up another load.

It was heavy. So incredibly heavy. On the last step, she gave up and collapsed, her bottom thumping down hard.

From behind her came Nathan's voice. "I heard you told Mrs. B that you and I slept together."

"Yes, well—" Her throat was tight. She tried to clear it. "I may have been exaggerating." Or maybe it had been wishful thinking.

"I heard you got kicked out of River Oaks."

She was going to cry. She couldn't. Not here. Not now. Not in front of him.

She took a deep, stabilizing breath. "No exaggeration there." It worked. Her voice barely trembled.

"You know what the B stands for, don't you?"

"I have a good idea."

"Let's just say it's not bitchin'."

He was trying to make her feel better about ever
thing. Instead, his attempt at kindness pushed her ov
the edge. Her vision blurred. Her throat tightened. S
jumped to her feet and ran for her car.

He must have been right behind her, because s
hadn't even opened the door when she felt hands on h
shoulders.

"Lark—"

Her breath shuddered in her chest as she kept h
face turned away, tears running down her cheeks. "
leave m-me a-lone."

"Aw, come on."

He coaxed her to him. She turned and his arms fold
around her. "You poor kid." She leaned into him, kno
ing she would regret this later, not caring. Right now
felt so right, so comforting.

He rocked her in his arms, against his chest. "You'
wiped out."

The fact that he knew, that he understood, made t
feel of his arms around her all the more welcome.

Her sobbing turned into little hiccups as she told hi
about her vandalized car. About her unsuccessf
attempt at wildlife photography. "I only got one pi
ture," she said, sniffling.

"Picture?" He was apparently having trouble follo
ing her.

"And it was of a finch. A common house finch!"
was much easier to wail over a bird than over the plig
of their two lives. "No mockingbird. No titmouse
raptor."

"If you want birds, I'll show you birds."

Her sniffles quieted. "You will?"

"Just two days ago, I saw a speckled grouse."

"*No.*"

"Yes."

She staggered as she tried to stand erect.

"Come on," he coaxed.

With his arm around her, they walked to the house. She was hardly aware of being led upstairs, hardly aware of being tucked into his bed. And as she fell asleep, hardly aware of the brush of his lips on her brow.

15

Lark woke up to the smell of food. Of food being cooked. Like eggs. Maybe even pancakes.

Since arriving in Elizabeth, she'd been living on a steady diet of yogurt, cereal, and cold sandwiches.

She was starving.

Dressed in yesterday's clothes—a wrinkled pair of jean shorts and a little white T-shirt with a row of buttons down the front—she made her way to the bathroom where she splashed cold water on her face, scrubbed her teeth with a washrag, and attempted to get the tangles out of her hair with a small black comb she found on the narrow shelf above the sink.

She finally gave up.

Barefoot, she skimmed down the wooden steps, bits of dirt and dust sticking to the soles of her feet as she went.

In the kitchen, the table was set.

With very old dishes, the kind somebody's grandmother

might use. There was a fork, knife, paper napkins. Orange juice. A stack of French toast.

She *loved* French toast.

Nathan stood in front of the ancient stove, wearing jeans and a T-shirt, spatula in hand, looking as if he knew what he was doing. He turned his head slightly, an acknowledgment of her arrival, then focused his attention back on the stove.

"Gonna be another hot one," he announced, as if they woke up in the same house everyday.

This was all too perfect. He was being too nice. First his bed, now breakfast.

"What's this all about?" she asked, bracing her hands on the top rung of a ladder-back chair.

"It's about fuel. It's about eating."

He cracked an egg on the side of the stove. Then, like someone attempting to open an oyster, he pried it in two. It hit the pan with a sizzle.

"As far as *how* they're fixed, well, it's a crap shoot."

Using the same awkward method he'd demonstrated with the first egg, he dropped three more into the skillet.

She pulled out the chair and sat down.

In front of the screen door, a box fan hummed, pulling in humidity and the sweet scent of morning dew. The air held the promise of another hot day, but at the moment, just past dawn, the temperature was bearable, even cozy.

Nathan slid two eggs onto her plate. Or at least she assumed they were the original two eggs. It was a little hard to tell, since they were now a cross between sunny-side up and scrambled. The fact that he hadn't presented her with a pair of perfectly cooked eggs was somehow endearing.

Nathan settled in the chair across from her.

Sunlight angled in low from the window above t
sink, illuminating the crop of unshaven hair along l
jawline, contouring the terrain, the landscape of his fac
intensifying the blueness of his eyes, shining off t
raven-wing blackness of his hair. Last night's sleep h
softened his face, giving him a look that was both se
and innocent.

"Thanks," she said, unfolding her napkin. "For letti
me stay here last night."

"You can stay as long as you want."

Was he inviting her to move in? Unthinkable. "I
going home today."

He shrugged as if to say, suit yourself. Then he pick
up his fork and sampled his cooking, pausing to pi
eggshell off his tongue. "I never had you figured for
quitter."

Truce over.

"Then you figured wrong. I'm a quitter from w
back. When I was little, I always wanted to be
Brownie. Two weeks of those ugly brown uniforms, a
I quit. A couple of years later, I took riding lessons.
month of being thrown on the ground, and I'd ha
enough. When I got into junior high, I thought I want
to learn how to play the piano. Didn't get past boo
two."

He laughed.

She'd meant for the stories to amuse him and distra
him, but she realized there was some truth to what she
said.

She *was* a quitter.

When they were done eating, he did his morni
chores, then he kept his promise and took her birding.

It wasn't until then that she noticed how different l

land was from his neighbors'. While it rolled and dipped in similar ways, his pastures weren't leveled. They didn't look as if some giant hand had completely wiped off every tree, every shrub, every fence post.

They ended up in a pasture she'd never been in before. One that was kind of tucked away between two hills. Running along two sides were wildlife strips. On some of the wooden fence posts were bluebird houses.

It was obvious that he cared about life.

And if that were so, then how could he have possibly killed anyone?

Sitting quietly at the edge of the pasture, near the wildlife strip, she was able to get a picture of a bluebird, and a flicker. A gray catbird and a cedar waxwing. And also one of a bird she couldn't identify, a bird so perfect it looked as if its wings had been painted with a brush.

Nathan leaned close, whispering, "That's a pine grosbeak."

She turned to ask him how he knew so much about birds. Her words died on her tongue. His face was just inches from hers. And in a trembling heartbeat, she knew she could lose herself in this man.

His lips moved. "I've never noticed that before."

The sun beat down on her head. Birds called from nearby trees. "What?" came her vague reply.

"You have freckles." He touched the bridge of her nose. "Right there."

She accidentally pressed the shutter-release button. The camera whirred, taking what would be a lovely close-up of her knee.

She pulled her gaze from his to unscrew the telephoto lens. Her hands shook as she packed the lens and camera in its case. She scrambled to her feet. "I think that's enough pictures. I'd better get going. Before it gets too late."

As they walked along a row of trees that led back to his house and her car, he paused, pulled down a branch from one of the trees, cutting it off with a pocketknife. If she didn't know better, he seemed intent on delaying her departure.

The branch was Y-shaped. With head bent, he trimmed the ends, folded the knife blade against his thigh, pocketed it, and asked, "Ever been dowsing?"

"Dowsing?"

"Yeah. You know. Water-witching. I'm a member of the A.S.D. American Society of Dowsers."

He was kidding. He had to be kidding. But she could see he wasn't. Maybe he did kill Mary Jane. "Never heard of that particular society," she admitted.

"Not everybody can do it," he explained.

Holding the branch parallel to the ground, he grasped two ends of the stick, with the single end pointing away from him, clenched palms up. "I don't know if it's a sixth sense, or maybe something in a person's physical makeup." He walked. Slowly.

Lark watched, her stomach sinking. He was crazy. Just like everybody said.

It was almost as if he forgot she was there. He seemed to be giving the stupid twig in his hands his total concentration. As she watched, feeling more disgusted by the minute, he started to shake. The muscles in his forearms bunched. His knuckles turned white.

And then the free end of the branch began to vibrate.

As Nathan hung on, acting as if he were fighting some unknown force, the branch began to move toward the ground, bending like a fishing pole. When the arch seemed so severe that it might break at any second, the twig shot toward the ground, with Nathan keeping a tight grip on the ends.

What a ridiculous display.

"There's an underground spring right here," he said in a breathless voice, as if the whole charade had tested his strength.

She readjusted the shoulder strap of her camera bag. "If you think I'm going to fall for something like that, then you are—"

She stopped short.

He lowered the stick. "What? Crazy? Is that what you were going to say?"

Exactly the word. "I was going to ask if you had any snake oil for sale."

He pressed his lips together in a tight line. Then, "You try it."

"I will not."

There were lines between his brows. Line at the corners of his mouth. He was mad! She couldn't believe he was mad. All because she didn't believe his little act.

Just when she started to like him, to think he might be human, he pulled something like this.

It was all for the best.

It would make him easier to forget.

She'd forgotten him already. The color of his eyes. His voice. His smile. The way he smelled, like outdoors.

Yes, she'd forgotten him already.

"Try it."

He stood in front of her, branch in hand.

"No."

"You can't just hold it limply in your hands." He demonstrated. "You have to take the ends like this, then give your wrists a twist."

"Ah." She nodded. "That's how you make it bend."

He shook his head, his anger still evident. "It bends *by itself.*"

"Then why isn't it bending now?"

"I don't know *why*. It probably has something to do with the electricity in a person's body. Something to do with positive and negative fields."

"Uh-huh." Sure.

He held the branch to her. "Try it."

"You said it didn't work with everybody."

"That's right."

"So if it doesn't work for me, then it won't prove any thing. Except that you're trying to make me look like a fool."

She took the branch. She stared at it. It was just a branch. Just green wood covered with tight bark.

It had been such a nice day. Why did he have to ruin it?

"Why are you doing this?" she asked.

He made a disgusted sound deep in his throat, grabbed the branch from her hand, and strode away.

"Have a nice life," he yelled over his shoulder. He spun around, walking backward as he talked. "Do you have faith in anything? Do you believe in anything without question?" Then he turned and strode away, quickly disappearing over a hill.

She thought about what he'd said. No, she supposed she didn't believe. Not anymore. Certainly not without question. Believing was another way of saying trust. And she trusted no one.

She moved in the direction of his house, catching her toe on the branch he'd thrown to the ground.

She bent over and picked it up.

Just a branch. Just a tree.

Do you believe in anything without question?

How had he said to hold it? Like this?

She grasped both ends. Then she twisted her wrists, creating tension in the entire branch.

She walked.

Slowly. One way. She turned and went the other.

Nothing. Just a stick in her hands.

She tried another direction.

And thought she felt a tingling in her palms.

Just her imagination. She tightened her grip. The tingling grew stronger. And then the tip of the branch began to move, began to bend toward the ground.

The force, the power, the pull, was so strong, it jerked the branch from her hands, leaving her palms stinging.

She stood there, staring at the now lifeless twig. She looked at her scraped palms. From there, her gaze moved in the direction Nathan had taken.

He was long gone.

She thought about some of the other things he'd told her, about electric fences and cattle whorls.

So the branch had moved. That didn't mean it had pointed to any water.

So what?

It had *moved*.

That was like communicating telepathically. Like bending a spoon with your mind.

When she got back to the house, there was no sign of him. His truck was gone. It was obvious he didn't want to have anything else to do with her.

She'd wanted to tell him it had worked. She'd wanted to tell him she was sorry she hadn't believed him.

But had it worked? Really?

Now that some time had passed, she wondered. Had she imagined it?

She looked at her palms. Red. Scraped.

She wondered . . .

She looked up at the two-story farmhouse, her gaze

falling on the second-story window, the place where Nathan grew his other cash crop.

She smiled to herself. There was something she was going to do before she left. Something very important.

16

Nathan pulled up in front of his house in time to see something fly out the upstairs bedroom window.

What the—?

Keeping his gaze directed at the upper story, he cut the engine, pulled the emergency brake, and got out. Beyond the window that was supposed to be closed but was now wide open, he saw nothing but darkness. He stood there a minute, hands on hips, watching.

Sure enough. As he waited, another dark object came hurtling out of that rectangular darkness.

What the—?

He caught a glimpse of blond hair.

Lark.

Caught a glimpse of a delicate arm.

Then something black was arcing through the air. It tumbled, the contents spilling, some of it falling straight to the ground, some drifting away on the breeze.

He stared, his mind fumbling.

His plants.

She was tossing out his damn plants!

In less than a second, he went from calm curiosity to blind rage. It roared through his veins. It filled his brain.

He didn't shout up at her. He didn't think about a plan of action. Suddenly he was running. Across the yard, the soles of his boots pounding up the wooden steps, keeping time with the anger boiling through him, keeping time with the pounding in his head.

Lark was ready to give the next to last tray a heave when she heard a sound.

Footsteps.

Heavy footsteps. Angry footsteps.

"Lark!"

She froze.

His voice was a deep, enraged shout, echoing up the stairwell.

Running footsteps.

On the stairs.

Anger.

Darkness.

Heat. Smothering heat.

Veiled, buried memories of another time came tumbling back, filling her mind, choking her.

Over the years, she'd fooled herself into thinking the memories were gone, that they'd been vanquished, left in her past, part of a person she used to be but was no longer.

She should have known better.

The memories hadn't been buried all that deep. Not deep at all. Instead, they'd been lurking just below the surface. Waiting, waiting.

The footsteps. Pounding, pounding. Getting closer, closer.

He burst into the room, the door slamming against the wall, his body a threatening silhouette in the opening, his anger radiating from him, touching her, filling the dark, confined room.

"What the hell are you doing?"

Her nerveless fingers dropped the tray. Dirt spilled on her clothes, her shoes, the plastic tray making a dull thump as it hit the floor. Her mouth moved, but no sound came out.

Run, she told herself. *Run.*

She tried. She really tried. But all she could manage was to shuffle backwards a few inches, her hip meeting up with the ledge of the open window.

He stormed across the room.

He grabbed her by both arms, his fingers digging into her flesh.

She could hardly feel anything. Fear filled her heart, her mind, her eyes.

He was shaking her, saying something, shouting at her.

She couldn't hear past the roaring in her head. She should say something, anything. She opened her mouth.

A sound—a wail, a pitiful sob tore from somewhere deep inside.

She stared up into his face, into the blue.

Keep your eyes on the blue.

Her heart pounded. Fear tasted like metal in her mouth. Panic-stricken words spilled from her, words that had been spoken years and years ago.

"Don't hurt me! Please don't hurt me!"

Shock waves recoiled through his blue eyes. And kept recoiling.

And then she dimly realized he was no longer holding her. His hands were in the air, palms out. His mouth was moving, speaking words she couldn't hear, his brows drawn together in pain or distress.

Sad eyes. She didn't remember the blue of his eyes being so sad.

Her hand bumped the window ledge behind her. She grasped it.

Nathan took a step toward her, one hand out, reaching.

She turned and dove through the open window.

"Lark!"

Nathan's anguished cry reverberated off the walls of the small farmhouse.

He lunged for the window.

It wasn't a straight drop to the ground. Two feet below the window was the pitched, shingled roof of the kitchen, where Lark now lay, huddled and shaking in fear. Fear of him.

She was so damn scared of him that she'd jumped out a two-story window.

"Lark—" His voice was a pained croak. It was all he could do to keep himself from crawling out on the roof with her and wrapping his arms around her. But *he* was what she feared. She thought he was going to kill her and toss her in the pond.

"Lark, stay where you are. I'm going to leave, okay? Do you hear me? I'm going to leave. And when I'm gone, I want you to climb back in the window, okay? Do you hear me?"

Her hair hid her face. He could see her ribcage rising and falling. To go out on the roof and struggle with her would put her in more danger than if she slid to the ground.

He watched, waited.

She didn't move.

"I'm leaving."

It was one of the hardest things he'd ever done, but he moved away from the window, walking backward. At the door of the bedroom, he stopped to listen.

Nothing.

"I'm going downstairs!"

And he did, making sure his feet fell hard and loud against the wooden steps, the sound echoing up to her.

Downstairs, he went out the kitchen door, letting it slam. In the yard, he looked up from where the dirt and trays were scattered on the ground. Lark was still lying on the roof, her face hidden.

He shouted up at her. "I'm leaving! When you hear my truck drive away, you know you'll be okay. Crawl back in the window after I'm gone."

No reaction.

He walked to his truck. He got in. He started the engine. And he slowly drove down the lane, away from his house, hoping she was paying attention to the performance he was staging for her benefit.

When he reached the end of the lane, he pulled to the side of the road and waited.

He waited for an hour.

He'd expected her to fly past in her little white car.

She never came.

So he got out of the truck and headed back in the direction he'd come.

He approached the house with care, noting that Lark's car was exactly where it had been earlier. Rounding the house, he looked up at the roof.

She was still there.

Only now she was sitting up, her back to the cornwhere the wall of the second story met the cupola. Eve
though the day was sweltering, her arms were wrappe
tightly around her, as if she were trying to keep warm.

She was staring at him.

He stuck his hands deep in the front pockets of hi
jeans. "Hi."

"Hi."

Her soft voice carried quietly toward him. The ton
held embarrassment.

"When I was little," he began conversationally, "
used to sit on the roof outside my bedroom window an
watch the sun go down."

No comment.

He would show her he was normal, not bent on mur
der. "I also used to go there whenever I got in troubl
for something."

She smiled a little at that.

"Then I started using it to sneak out."

She smiled a little more.

Thus encouraged, he asked, "Can I come up?"

A pause. A blink. Then a nod.

On the way, he stopped by the refrigerator.

Not much in it but milk and eggs. Some bacon. A cou
ple of beers. He checked the cupboard, and finall
dredged up a ziplock bag full of sunflower seeds. H
tucked them in his back pocket and headed upstairs.

He was careful not to startle her when he got to th
window.

He ducked his head and crawled through. With knee
bent, the soles of his boots braced against the slante
roof, he approached to finally settle down beside he
keeping a good two feet between them.

Out past the roof, past the fields that were now turning green with this year's new crop, was the sun, suspended in the sky, a brilliant red.

He leaned to one side, reached into the back pocket of his jeans, and pulled out the plastic bag. "Sunflower seeds?" he asked, extending the open bag.

She didn't seem to quite understand his question.

He shook the bag. "Fixed 'em myself. Soak 'em overnight in saltwater, then bake 'em."

She held out her hand. Her palm was scraped, dirty from the potting soil.

And then he noticed that both of her knees were scraped.

He wanted to scoop her up into his arms and hold her tight, protect her, take her someplace safer than a roof. Instead, with a somewhat unsteady hand, he poured some sunflower seeds into her cupped palm.

And so they watched the sun go down while they munched on soggy sunflower seeds.

"I'm sorry about your plants."

"That's okay." He picked some beggar's lice off his jeans, giving the barbed seeds a toss. "It doesn't matter." Five years of work down the drain, but it didn't matter.

"I thought maybe . . ." She sniffled, then wiped at her nose with the back of her hand. "I thought the police might come. I thought they might find your plants. I'm sorry. It was none of my business."

"Lark, it doesn't matter." The plants were gone. It was over. Done.

The sun went down behind the town of Elizabeth. Down past the grain elevator, and the church steeple.

She pulled in a trembling breath. "How does a person get so drunk that he can't remember anything?"

"Easy. Too easy."

"Oh."

The vagueness in her voice told him she didn't get
No, she probably wouldn't understand. She'd proba
never tied one on like that, never let herself get to t
point of total shut-down.

"I used to drink. A lot." May as well come clean. "Th
one day I woke up and realized I had a problem. That
better get my act together. So I quit. Until the night
Mary Jane's death, I hadn't been wasted in years.

"I must have blacked out. All I know is that I woke
on my front porch the next morning. And I could
remember anything." He closed the bag of sunflow
seeds and put them back in his pocket.

An ugly story. One he certainly wasn't proud of.

Darkness was nearing completion. The automa
yard light came on, the filament humming, bugs imm
diately swarming. At ground level, crickets chirped. (
in the distance, near the pond, he could hear the cr
of frogs. And closer, hidden in the leaves of the tre
cicadas whirred.

"I'm sorry I scared you," he said. "I shouldn't ha
come tearing up here like that."

"It isn't you. It's me." She wouldn't look at hi
Instead, she picked nervously at the hem of her sho
"I was raped."

His heart stopped beating.

Raped.

He thought she was afraid of him because of what h
happened to Mary Jane. He'd never imagined . . . b
then he remembered the night in the stream, how h
kissed her and she'd flipped out.

Oh God. Lark.

He wished he could do something, wished he co
somehow change the past, erase it.

"It was a long time ago. But sometimes . . . sometimes it seems like it just happened."

He heard her swallow.

"About ten years ago, I was going to college in Texas. I'd seen him in one of my classes, but we'd never spoken. I lived on campus, in a little efficiency apartment. One night, he followed me home."

She stopped, pulled in a deep breath, then continued. "He, um, he had a knife. And when . . . when he was done, he tried to kill me."

He didn't know if he wanted to hear anymore, didn't know if he could handle it. He hadn't cried in years, but suddenly he felt an old pain in his throat, a burning in his eyes.

"When I could leave the hospital, I went home to California, back to my parents. And that's where I've been ever since. Until now. Working for my father, out of my parents' home."

No wonder she didn't seem to know much about the world. She'd spent the last ten years locked safely away from it.

"Ah, Lark." His voice held all of his despair, all of his regret. "I'm sorry. I'm so sorry."

They were both quiet. Then her voice came to him through the gathering darkness. "Would you do something for me?"

He waited.

"Would you hold my hand?"

He wanted to hold all of her, but for the moment, her hand would do. He took it, careful of her scraped palm.

"Would you do something else?"

"You name it."

"Would you make love to me?"

17

Her words hung between them in the echoi
silence. Lark felt heat burning her face, making her g
of the darkness, glad Nathan couldn't see the red flu
staining her cheeks.

Seconds passed, and still there was no response fro
Nathan. How humiliating. She wished she could take
all back, wished she could erase the last five minutes.

Her throat was tight. She swallowed, but it didn't
any good. The silence was more than she could sta
She had to do something, even if it meant filling it w
incoherent babble. And really, what better to fill silen
with? Incoherent babble could be very comforting, p
fect for just such a situation.

"When I was little," she began, keeping her eyes
some point in the distance, beyond the windmill, "I us
to be afraid to walk past this certain house. I would cr
the street to avoid it. It was tiny, with a sharply pitche
dark-green roof. The yard was a tangle of weeds. I w

sure a witch lived there. I thought if I got too close, she would grab me and pull me inside."

Lark ran a tongue across dry lips, the fingers of one hand twisting the hem of her shorts.

Talking calmed her. And as she talked, she began to notice things. The lightning bugs. The crickets. The half moon. Even though the day had been suffocatingly hot, the night was beautiful.

"One day my father made me go to the house. To meet her. The witch. I was terrified. I begged him not to take me, but he wouldn't listen.

"It turned out that the lady who lived there was blind. She served us tea and cookies. We used the most delicate-looking china I'd ever seen." Lark smiled, wistful at the memory. "The cup she gave me had red lipstick on the rim. That made me sad, because I knew she would never have wanted to give a guest a cup with lipstick on it, not if she'd known it was there.

"When we left, she handed me a bouquet of violets."

That was it. The end of her story. The end of her babbling. She really didn't know why she'd told him the story at all.

"Everybody's afraid of something," he said.

How true. "What are you afraid of?" She found the idea intriguing.

"You scared the hell out of me when I saw you jump out that window."

What had she expected from him? Some deep, dark confession? Men didn't talk about such things. It wasn't their way.

"Lark, I'm not trying to be a smart-ass, but have you tried counseling? I think something like that is more what you need."

Memories avalanched into one condensed version of

the last ten years. All the hours spent sitting on the other side of Dr. Mary Sweeney's desk, talking and talking and talking. Today had proven that it had gotten her nowhere. She was just as afraid of men now as she'd been those awful hours, awful days, awful weeks following her attack.

"Oh yes."

For possibly the first time in his life, Nathan found himself at a total loss. He didn't have a clue how to deal with Lark. He only knew the bleakness of her answer told him more than he wanted to know.

Did he want to make love to her?

Hell yes.

But not like this. It would be nothing more than taking advantage of her. It would make him the lowest of the low. And it would once again make her a victim.

He got to his feet, bracing the sole of his boots against the slant of the roof, his thigh muscles tense. He held out a hand. "Come on." His voice was low and soft and coaxing, infused with qualities he didn't recognize in himself.

His only plan was to get her off the roof, get her to a safer place.

His work-roughened fingertips touched the softness of her arm, lightly, without pressure. "Let's go inside."

She surprised him by putting her hand in his, by letting him help her up.

Earlier, she'd boldly hurtled herself out the window. Now, she remained in a crouched position, as if afraid that standing might throw her off balance. Now, she hugged the side of the house, proof of just how much he'd scared her before.

They inched their way to the window. He felt the trembling in her body as he helped her through the opening.

Inside, he turned on the light, revealing remnants of his evil, decadent work, now nothing more than black dirt scattered across the wooden floor. His heart dropped. All the time invested. For nothing.

It hurt.

More than he'd thought it would. That surprised him. He didn't think he'd cared about anything anymore.

She thought she was helping him. That was funny. Funny in a painful sort of way.

He looked up to find her watching him with big, frightened eyes. At that moment, all he wanted was to wrap his arms around her. He wanted to carry her to his bed, which beckoned from just yards away. He wanted to gently and patiently remove her clothes, one item at a time. He wanted to love her. Love her the way a woman should be loved.

Tenderly.

Slowly.

Reverently.

Oh how he wanted to love her.

But he couldn't be her redemption. He couldn't be anybody's answer to a screwed-up problem.

He just wanted to feel her under him. That was all. No strings attached. If they made love for anything more than mutual pleasure, then that would create some kind of bond. That was the last thing he needed.

Instead of touching her, he took a step back.

She didn't miss his quick retreat. Shame filled her eyes. Color drained from her face.

"Look—" He wanted to explain that it wasn't her. It was the whole damn screwed-up situation. This was new to him. It wasn't everyday a woman asked him to help her get over her fear of sex. It was hard to know how to handle such a delicate matter.

He was still struggling to formulate an excuse that wouldn't send her over the edge, when she took off.

She ran to the bathroom, slamming the door behind her. Or at least she tried to slam the door. The wood was swollen from the weeks of high humidity, and now it wouldn't shut all the way.

He heard her throw her weight against it in a futile attempt to get door to meet jamb. No good. She must have given up, because the next thing he heard was the sound of running water.

He gave her five minutes, then he knocked on the door. "Lark?"

She didn't answer.

He tried again.

Again no answer.

He grasped the glass knob, turned it, and threw his shoulder against the door. With a shudder, the door came unstuck and he went stumbling into the bathroom, coming to a halt where Lark sat on the curled edge of the clawfoot tub, staring straight ahead, her hands clasped between her knees.

She'd been crying. He could tell that right away. Dirt and tears never mixed well. She'd rubbed her face with the same hands she'd used to toss out his plants. There were smudges on her cheeks, her chin, under her eyes.

She didn't move. Didn't blink. Didn't give any indication he'd just tumbled into the room. Then, without looking up, without changing a single inflection in her voice, she said, "I'd better leave."

God, woman. Don't do this to me.

He dug out a clean washcloth from the laundry basket on the floor. He wet it with warm water from the sink. Then he turned back to her.

He positioned himself so he stood between her knees.

With the washcloth, he slowly stroked the dirt from her face, first one cheek, then the other.

He finished and tossed the dirty washcloth in the bathtub. Throughout their rather intimate encounter, there had been no reaction from her whatsoever.

"I'm tainted."

The same monotone voice she'd used earlier.

"What?" He thought he couldn't have heard right.

"Tainted. Dirty. That's why you don't want to . . . touch me. I don't blame you. What happened wasn't my fault, but it left a stain no matter who's fault it was. And when you wear that stain for years and years . . . well, it becomes a part of you."

"Christ, Lark. Don't say that."

"After it happened, I couldn't take enough baths. Do you know, I used to scrub my skin until it bled. But no matter what I did—" She looked up at him with hollow eyes. "I never felt clean."

Up until that moment, he'd hung back. He'd tried to keep an emotional distance. That was over.

"When I first saw you, do you know what I thought?"

She didn't respond. He had no way of knowing if she was even listening.

"You looked so pure, so untouched. Like somebody from another world. Another time."

"That was before you knew about me."

"You're no different today than you were then."

She shook her head. A wry smile briefly touched her lips. "I saw your reaction. You didn't want to touch me. You were repelled."

He crouched down in front of her, his hands grasping her knees. His next words came slowly, clearly, filled with a sincerity he hoped she'd recognize. "You asked me what I was afraid of. You. I'm afraid of you. I didn't touch you because I was afraid I wouldn't want to stop touching you."

Her head came up. To his relief, some of the bleakness had left her eyes. He could see she wanted to believe him, but didn't quite dare. "No." she said.

"Yes. I'm afraid of *you*."

"Why?"

"I can't be anybody's salvation."

She put a palm to his cheek, a gesture of aching tenderness. "Why not?"

Why not? So simple. Like a child asking why the sky is blue.

"Would you do something for me before I leave?" she asked, getting to her feet, grasping his hand, tugging him up after her. "Would you kiss me?"

If he kissed her, it would be more than a kiss. There was more involved than lips touching lips. There were souls involved. And that scared him. Scared the hell out of him. "I don't think that's a good idea."

"Do you want to?"

He groaned. "God yes."

"Then do it."

The top of her head came to his chin. She had to tilt her face to look at him. And with her eyes, she begged him. Not to embarrass her. Not to turn her away. Her lips, swollen and red from crying, were the sweetest of invitations. And in that second, he understood a little of what she wanted from him.

Why him? Why not somebody with his act together? Why did she think he was the one to chase away her demons? He couldn't even handle his own.

"I want to know how it feels."

He had a pretty good idea how it would feel.

But in the end, he discovered he didn't have a clue.

When it came to Lark, everything was new. Not a rebirth, but new. Brand new.

Nothing he'd ever known prepared him for the seductive feel of her lips under his. She was all trembling, swollen softness. She was a delicate quivering breath against his lips. She was warmth. She was the sweet scent of green, of the mysterious plants that grew wild in the tangle of bittersweet just beyond the hedgerow. She was the flutter of life deep within his lonely soul.

He'd had every right to be afraid.

With his legs braced, he pulled her up taut against him, savoring the feel of her firm soft body next to his.

The first time he'd seen her, she'd come floating across his field, caught in the shimmering waves of heat rising from the rich earth. At that time, he'd wondered if she was real, wondered if he was hallucinating. This was no hallucination, yet he had the same feeling, the same sense of whimsy, of ephemerality. He was afraid that if he didn't hold her tightly enough, she might disappear.

They would make love. They had to make love. He had to know this woman, body and soul. He had to know her fears, and her passions. Not only know her, but somehow, in some small way, become her.

Almost as if she'd read his mind, she asked, "Do you believe in destiny?"

"Destiny?" The word conjured up images of people who slept with pyramids under their beds. People who fondled rocks. "Nah."

"I never thought I did. But now . . . I don't know. I came to Metamora County thinking I was running away again. Like I've always run away. Instead I met you."

"I'm nobody's destiny. Don't go thinking that."

"You could make me better."

Her words rocked him, scared him even more. "That's

a lot to put on a guy." He needed to set things straight. "I can't promise you anything. I'm *not* promising you anything."

"I don't want your promises."

"Good. That's good."

Thus reassured, he inhaled, pulling the scent of her deep into his lungs. Hand to her head, his fingers sifted through her hair, letting satiny strands slide across his wrist. "It might hurt," he warned softly.

"It already hurts." She took his hand and put it to her heart. "Here." She moved it down, his hand splayed across her belly. "And here."

His heart was pounding in his ears. His breathing was already becoming irregular. "I don't want to hurt you."

A smile touched her lips, and there was no fear in her eyes. "I know." Then suddenly she seemed self-conscious again. "I have another confession."

Oh God. How much more could he handle?

"I'm not taking anything."

"Taking anything?" he asked blankly.

"Birth control." She swallowed nervously. "For a while there, I had some birth control pills. I thought maybe, someday . . . but then they expired and I threw them out. And I never got any more." Then she added quietly, so quietly that he almost didn't hear. "That was years ago."

"Don't worry," he said, rocking her in his arms, against his chest, wondering what the hell he was letting himself in for, wondering why his heart was singing about it. "I'll take care of you."

18

He quit fighting.

Maybe it was giving up, or giving in. Didn't matter. Not at the moment anyway. Because this was about now. Not yesterday. Not tomorrow. Now. And right now, he just wanted to lose himself in Lark.

The bathroom, with its cold porcelain tub and hard linoleum floor, was no place to make love. So he coaxed her into the bedroom, where they halted just inside the door. He reached for the wall switch, flicking on the glaring ceiling light. Both of them stared at the plump mattress with its tangle of white cotton sheets. Tumbling to the floor was a quilt his grandmother had made, with geometric patterns that had always made him think of an aerial view of cropland. Log cabin, or some such thing she'd called its design.

The room was suffocatingly hot, still holding the humid heat of the day. At one time, Nathan had owned a window air conditioner, but it bit the dust and now resided at the bottom of some landfill.

He crossed the room to open the window, the sound of his footfall echoing hollowly.

Window open, night air whispered in. Heavy. Humid. Smelling of damp earth and green vegetation. Even though the outside temperature was around eighty, the fresh air felt cool against his hot skin.

An orchestra of sounds lent their own atmosphere. Cicadas whirred in the nearby maple. Crickets called from their hiding place in the tall grass that lined the base of the house.

Nathan picked up a length of broken yardstick and propped open the heavy window. It was unnerving as hell when the window came crashing shut in the middle of the night. Twice he'd been awakened to a sound similar to a shotgun going off a foot from his head. That was all it had taken to send him stumbling through the dark, looking for some sort of prop.

Window secure, he turned on the box fan.

"Not exactly five-star accommodations," he told Lark, who was still hovering anxiously near the door. "Sorry."

Had she changed her mind? Ten minutes ago, he would have cheered such a decision. Now he just might break down and weep.

She was looking around, checking out the room.

Not a whole helluva lot to see. A ceiling light full of dead bugs.

Gotta clean that one of these days.

Flowered wallpaper that had probably been hung twenty or thirty years ago. Under it was probably more flowered wallpaper. And under that, more flowered wallpaper.

The floor was bare wood. There was a double bed. A dresser that was almost empty. A pile of clothes. That was about it.

Thumbing through copies of *House Beautiful* just hadn't been one of his priorities. But now that he looked at the room, now that he imagined seeing it though Lark's eyes, he was a little ashamed. The word *squalor* came to mind.

Her gaze came back to focus on him. She smiled, and he thought he detected a slight tremble to her lips. But her voice was strong, confident.

"I like it."

"You do?"

Was she kidding? Trying to make him feel good?

"It has character."

"Yeah, but what kind of character? I'm thinking the guy in *Animal House*. The one John Belushi played."

She smiled. "No." She laughed.

This was going very well. Laughter was good.

"I was thinking more like quaint."

"Quaint?" He did a little double take bob of the head. Not backing down, she nodded.

Quaint.

How about that. It was a word he associated with old ladies, with old maids. With mothballs and doilies. With soft blue hair and crookedly applied red lipstick. With those print aprons that wrapped around a woman like a baby's bib. What were those all about?

"Quaint."

The more he thought about it, the more he liked it. He smiled and began to move slowly toward her. "I've never been associated with quaint before. Pigsty, yes. Quaint, no."

Her smile grew.

This was good. This was very good.

But still she continued to hover near the door, as if ready to bolt at any second. Now that he was closer, now that he was standing directly in front of her, he could see the sheen of perspiration above her lip, could see the flutter of a pulse in her neck.

She was scared.

Her gaze traveled to the bed, then quickly scooted away. "I, uh . . ." She clasped and unclasped her hands. She shifted from one foot to the other. "I never felt really comfortable about my body." She waved a hand in the air. As she spoke, she kept her head slanted to one side.

Endearing was a word Nathan had never used in his life, but Lark was becoming more endearing by the second.

"I mean, I never liked to undress in front of people. I never even like to be seen in my underwear." She let out a shaky, self-conscious laugh that wasn't really a laugh at all but a bad case of nerves. Both hands shot up, them returned to the tightly clasped position. "I always said, if a baby could be born with clothes on, that would be me. I'm kind of, well, straight up and down. Boy's pants always fit me better than women's." Like someone directing a parking aircraft, she made a choppy motion with both hands.

Her revealing, engaging confession caused him to kind of fall apart inside, caused him to experience a tenderness that was a hurt, an ache that wouldn't go away.

"Lark—"

She didn't wait for him to continue. She started to rattle on and on, going over the same territory.

"Lark—"

Hands going. Talking, talking, talking.

"Lark—"

He grasped her by both arms. Her mouth stopped moving and she looked up at him, her expression kind of startled, kind of bemused. Kind of like she'd forgotten he was even in the room.

"Lark, I have to ask you something. Have you ever done this before? I mean, before . . . before you were—"

He didn't want to ignore the issue, yet he didn't know if this was the time to bring up her rape. With one word, she saved him from having to make a decision.

"No."

Lord.

He tilted his head to the ceiling. He looked at the bugs in the light. He looked at the flowered walls. This was way too much for him. Way more than he'd bargained for.

"Lark, I don't think I'm the one for this."

"Do you know somebody else who is?"

He hoped she was kidding.

"Well?"

He didn't want to think of her with anybody else. Hell, he'd gotten mad just knowing she'd gone out with that geek Brett Gillette.

She leaned into him, not in a sexy, I'm-going-to-turn-you-on way, but a way that showed she didn't fear him anymore, at least not too much.

"You're the one."

Her voice was a husky whisper that sent goose bumps across his forearms.

And he thought, *Maybe I am.*

And standing there looking at her, he felt awkward, felt like this was his first time. If he bombed, if he said the wrong thing, did the wrong thing, well . . . maybe it would really mess up her head. He certainly didn't want to be responsible for her mental health.

"You'll have to help me. You'll have to tell me what to do."

Jeez. The line was from a horny man's dream. And yet he couldn't quiet a voice that kept telling him to go jump in a cold stream and forget about it.

"Are you sure about this?" he asked.

"Positive. We just have to have a plan, that's all."

She was talking fast again, her words coming out in a breathless rush.

"We have to have some idea of how to go about it. I just have to know what's happening. What to expect. What I'm supposed to do."

The voice in his head fell silent. No more arguments. This was it. He was going to be with Lark. He braced his legs apart and pulled her to him. Then he reached behind her and turned off the light. "That's the thing about sex," he said. "There really is no plan. No book of rules."

"Dark," she said. "Dark is good."

He walked backward, pulling her after him, toward the bed. Moonlight spilled in the open window, falling across the mattress, leaving a rectangular pattern of light on the floor.

They sat down, side by side, the bed dipping, his right arm pressing against her left.

And they sat.

"Now what?" she asked.

"How about we start with our shoes?"

"Oh, that's a good idea. A very good idea."

She quickly toed off her little slip-on shoes while he bent over, unhooked the speed laces on his workboots, then went through the usual tugging ritual, dropping them to the floor one at a time. Those were quickly followed by gray socks that had once been white.

Sorting his laundry. It was something else he needed to work on.

They both sat there some more, side by side.

"Shirts?" he asked.

She jumped. "W-what?"

"How about we take off our shirts?"

"Oh. Okay."

He crossed his arms, grasped the hem of his faded T-shirt, and tugged it over his head, dropping it to the floor with his boots.

He turned to find her still struggling with the buttons of her white cotton top. He gently brushed her hands away. "Let me."

The buttons were tiny and close together. He thought he'd never get to the last one. Finally he was done. He spread her blouse open, revealing pale breasts overflowing from white lace. He slid the blouse down her arms, until she sat there in the moonlight wearing nothing but her shorts and bra. And her hair. It was almost like clothing, it was so long, so full, giving him tantalizing glimpses of a body that was slight and firm.

He wanted to see more of her. Needed to see more of her.

With both hands, he reached behind her, unfastened the hooks of her bra, then slid the garment down her arms to join his clothes on the floor.

Entranced, bemused, captivated, he stroked his thumbs across her velvet nipples, then filled his palms with the weight of her breasts.

She didn't move.

She seemed to be holding her breath.

He brought a hand up, cupping her chin. With his other hand supporting her back, his fingers against her bare skin, he lowered his head until his lips found hers.

Her mouth opened under his, warm and welcoming. He felt her hands on his biceps as she sank back against the mattress, pulling him after her. Against the damp skin of his chest, he felt the soft mounds of her breasts, felt the pliancy of her nipples, felt himself grow harder. Briefly he pulled away. If he was going to ever get out of his jeans, it would have to be now.

He peeled them off his damp body, the fan in the corner continued to hum, the air caressing and cooling his fevered skin. He looked up to see Lark watching him in the moonlight, her eyes round, curious. He could feel his arousal, stiff and hard and aching beneath the cloth of his boxer shorts.

May as well go for it.

He shucked his remaining clothes, leaving him totally exposed to her eyes.

Slowly, she sat up.

This was it. She was leaving. He'd scared her away with a hard-on as stiff and big as a post.

But instead of leaving, she reached out . . . and she touched him.

Air hissed through his teeth.

She touched him again, two fingers moving lightly down his shaft, then back. Examining. Memorizing. Tantalizing.

Torturing.

"You're awfully big. I don't know . . ." Her voice held wonder. Surprise. "And so hot."

He squeezed his eyes shut and let out a groan.

"Soft," she said, her voice breathless, surprised. "Like velvet. But hard at the same time."

He may have made another sound, because she asked, "Does it hurt?"

He didn't know if he could answer. Blood pounded through his veins, in his ears. Sweat ran down his spine. "Yes," he finally managed to grind out.

Her hand sprang away. "I'm sorry."

"No," he gasped, taking her hand, moving it back. "It's a good—" He swallowed, "a good kind of hurt."

She continued to cradle him, to stroke him and hold him while he stood there, afraid to move, afraid to breathe, afraid to touch her in return. There was an innocence about her curiosity, like a child examining a flower. The only difference was she was playing with a loaded gun.

He'd almost reached the point of losing it, almost reached the point where he had to stop her before he spilled himself in her hands, when she quit her erotic administrations. Then, while he gasped for air and tried to pull himself together, she casually unbuttoned and unzipped her pants, quickly stripping down to nothing. Then she lay back across the mattress. For a moment, he just stood there, drinking in her smooth-skinned beauty.

"I'm ready."

Her arms were at her sides, legs straight, thighs press tightly together, eyes squeezed shut.

That took some of the steel out of him.

He let out a sigh. "Lark, I think you need to learn that half the pleasure is getting there."

Her eyes came open and she regarded him from her sacrificial position on the bed. "It is?"

"It is."

She was silent a moment, absorbing everything. Was it his imagination, or did her body relax slightly?

"Show me."

She pushed herself up, so she was kneeling on the edge of the bed, her long moonlight-kissed hair falling over her shoulder, partially covering her nakedness. And he didn't know if he'd ever seen such a beautiful, alluring sight. And he told her so, in a choked, passion-filled voice.

"Nathan, teach me to like it."

That was it. They should just go about it like a lesson. The way he might teach someone to plant a field. Straightforward. You do this. Then you do this. Then this.

He ran his fingers through her hair, working his way to the very ends, letting the strands sift across his arm, letting it fan from his fingers to her thigh. "The most important part," he said in an enthralled voice, hypnotized by the shimmering spectacle, "is what happens before. The preparation." With the back of both hands, he lifted her hair, draping it behind her shoulders, exposing her body to his gaze. Beautiful. God, she was so beautiful. She stole his breath.

He struggled to bring his thoughts back around, struggled to focus. "You can put seed in the ground, but if you haven't done everything right, it doesn't matter. It's just wasted time."

Her eyes went from his face, to his chest, to his erection, which was just below eye level, back to his chest. She reached up and touched him, a light skimming of her fingers across the padded flesh of his chest. She touched one hard nipple, then the other. She slid a knuckle down the indentation than ran to his navel.

"I'm not sure I like that analogy," she said, sounding as if she too were having trouble concentrating. "I'm not a field waiting to be planted."

"But if you were . . ."

"If I was . . ."

"What would you do?"

Good. She'd decided to play the game. "I'd wait until the time was right. Until the time was perfect."

"Yeah?"

"Yeah."

A cloud drifted across the moon and the room grew dark as an eclipse.

In the darkness, Nathan felt Lark's hands on the backs of his thighs, then he felt her hot cheek, brushing his erection.

"Nathan?"

He plunged his fingers through her hair, to her scalp, cradling her head. "What, love?" His voice was a hoarse croak. If he could die right now, he'd be happy.

"I'm ready. Really ready this time."

"G-good."

He had talked about taking it slow, but suddenly she had him so hot he didn't know how much longer he could hold out.

He didn't want to leave her, didn't want to move away from her soft, hot, tender touch, but he'd promised to protect her, to take care of her.

"Sweetheart—"

She was moving her face back and forth, rubbing her cheek against him. He could feel her soft hair, brushing his thighs, feel her small fingers gripping the backs of his legs.

"Sweetheart—" he repeated.

"Mmm?"

"Hang on. Hold that thought. I have to get a rubber."

They separated with great reluctance. Long enough for him to pull open a drawer of the bedside stand, feel for a packet, open it, and slip the latex into place. Then he was tumbling her backward on the mattress, his lips finding hers in the darkness, his hands finding her breasts, her belly, the wet, damp heat between her thighs.

"Ah, Lark. You are the sweetest thing. An angel. A sweet, sweet gift from heaven."

He tested her. She was hot and wet. All his promises

to go slow dissolved. He hadn't known it would be like this. He hadn't known she'd take him so close to the edge. So close to losing control. *He* had planned to do the taking. He had planned to do the showing. Now everything was turned around.

"Lark—" He smoothed her hair, soaked with sweat, back from her brow. "Lark, are you ready?"

He lifted his hips, poised between her sweet thighs. "Lark?" His arms were trembling. "Are you ready?"

A hesitation. Then he felt her hands on his buttocks, her fingers digging into his flesh. "Yes."

He had to fight to keep from plunging deep inside her. Instead, he entered her very slowly.

She was tight. And hot. Like a furnace.

And small. He wasn't sure he could achieve full penetration.

He moved, careful to keep his stroke shallow, his heartbeat erratic, his breathing quick. Beneath him, he could feel the tenseness of her body, as if she were suddenly rejecting him.

"Relax, Lark. You have to relax."

"I can't." It was almost a sob.

"Shhh." He blew against her perspiring brow.

"*I can't.* There's something wrong. It's not going to work. It's me. I can't . . . I can't—"

Her breath was coming in short gasps. He could sense the panic building in her.

And then it hit him. In the dark, he could be anybody. In the dark, he could be a rapist.

With his left hand, he quickly reached up and turned on the bedside lamp, the light practically blinding him. Beneath him, Lark lay with her eyes squeezed shut, her face turned away, a knuckled hand to her mouth, as if holding in a scream.

"Lark, Lark." He grasped her chin. He pulled her face around. "Look at me. Open your eyes and look at me."

Her eyes blindly searched, then found him, locking in.

"*Nathan.*"

He saw the recognition in her face, heard the relief in her voice.

And something bloomed, something blossomed in his chest.

Love?

He hoped to hell it wasn't love.

"Thatta girl." He continued to smooth her hair, his fingers at her temple. "It's okay."

They were soaked with sweat, as if they'd taken a double steambath.

Under him, he could feel her begin to relax, feel the tightness leave her muscles. He brought his face down and brushed his lips across hers.

Softly.

Lightly.

Lingeringly.

Slowly, her mouth opened under his. As he deepened his kiss, he also deepened his penetration. And this time, her body welcomed him, took him.

He broke the kiss, lifting his face so he could look into her eyes. "Okay?"

That one word was all he could manage at the moment. Blood thundered in his ears, his heart hammered in his chest as he fought the urge to bury himself deeper, as he fought the urge to pull her tightly against him and thrust himself into her again and again.

She blinked and nodded. Her face was flushed, her eyes swollen from his kisses. The hair at her temple was damp and dark.

Lark. Sweet, sweet Lark.

He wanted to kiss her again, but he knew she needed to keep her eyes on his face. "Look at me," he managed to say. "Just watch me."

She nodded, keeping her eyes locked to his, as if there was something in him she needed. As if he somehow gave her strength. That knowledge made him experience a tenderness he'd never experienced before.

"Okay?"

She nodded. "Okay."

"I'm going to . . . move . . . a little." He lifted himself away, almost all the way out. Then, as he kept his eyes on her face, he slowly, slowly sank inside her.

Her expression was the most erotic thing he'd ever seen. Her eyes widened, then, as his penetration deepened, her lids fluttered closed, her swollen lips became slack. A small sound of surprised pleasure escaped her. The next time he withdrew completely, then entered her again, stroking her small bud as he moved against her, watching her face, watching the passion building within her.

She began making small, keening sounds. She said his name, over and over and over. He'd never experienced anything like this, anything remotely close. It was so new, so wonderful, so . . .

His name was a cry. And then she shuddered against him.

He thrust. Once. Twice. Long. Deep.

He felt her contract around him, again and again, milking him until he collapsed weakly against her.

19

Oh, wow.

The words kept bouncing around in Lark's head.

Oh, wow.

She'd never known. Hadn't had a clue it could be this way.

It was true. Things happen when you least expect them. She hadn't been expecting anything enjoyable. She'd planned on it being like medicine. Something done for her own good.

But this . . . *this.*

Wow.

Nathan lay spent on top of her, his breathing ragged, his body limp, as if he'd just run a marathon. She could still feel him inside her, not as large, but there, a part of her.

This sort of thing could be the downfall of society, she decided. It was amazing anybody left their homes when there was something this wonderful to be doing. She didn't want this moment, this feeling to end, didn't want him to leave.

But then he was pushing himself up, withdrawing from her. Air moved against her hot damp skin. The bed dipped. In the lamplight, he got up.

And left.

Just like that.

Without a word. Without a kiss.

Well, what had she expected? It wasn't like they were in love. It wasn't like she'd asked him to hold her afterwards. She'd asked him to help her get over her fear of sex. That was it. That was all.

The light was too bright. Blinding. She reached out and turned it off. She should get up. She should get her clothes.

She should go. *Leave.*

Go where? She didn't have any place *to go.* It was the middle of the night.

Tears stung her eyes.

Great. Now she was going to feel sorry for herself. How ridiculous.

Grow up.

What had she expected? For him to cuddle with her, hold her tenderly within the circle of his strong, protective arms?

Of course.

What she needed to do was get her clothes on, tell him thanks for the lesson, and breeze out of there. Why, he was probably *waiting* for her to leave right now. Probably wondering what she was doing, dillydallying around in his bed when he wanted to get to sleep.

And then she had a *really* horrid thought. He'd probably hated it.

Earlier, when they'd gone through the awkwardness

of shedding their clothes, she'd thought how nice it would have been if they'd just magically fallen off the way they did in books. Now she wished they'd magically go back on her body where they belonged. She didn't want to get caught half naked, struggling back into her clothes, looking like a deer captured in the headlights.

She was trying to pick up her panties with her toes when she heard a sound in the hallway.

Quickly, she grabbed a corner of the tangled sheet, pulled it over her, and turned her face to the window, her back to the door.

Behind her, the bed dipped. Out the window, she could see stars. The clouds that had earlier obliterated the moon had moved on. Moonlight once again poured across the bed. She pressed the cool sheet against her hot face, wishing she'd gotten up and gotten her clothes on when she'd had the chance.

She was just no good at the sex stuff. It was too hard. Too complicated.

"Hey," she said, her voice only slightly quivery. "Thanks." That sounded okay. That sounded fine.

"Thanks?"

"I think I'm cured."

"Oh yeah?"

She detected a teasing quality in his voice. Good. He hadn't picked up on her mood. "Yeah."

"I know more remedies."

What? What did he mean by that?

She rolled over so she could look at him. "Is that right?" she asked, playing for time, trying to figure this out.

"Yeah." He held up a plastic cup, the kind they gave away at fast food restaurants. "Wanna drink?"

"I don't drink."

"It's water."

"Oh."

Did she ever feel stupid. "Sure." She took the cup. So that's where he'd gone. Maybe he hadn't been so eager to get away from her after all. She took a sip. The water was ice cold. Good.

Some *after* would have been nice, she thought, handing the cup back to him. He was so big on what happened before. Some after would have been nice.

He downed the rest of the water and put the empty cup on the dresser. Then he slid under the sheet and reached for her, his hand settling on her hip, sending a wave of what she now recognized as desire through her.

He wants to do it again.

That's what this was all about.

In the moonlight, she looked at him.

He was beautiful. Rugged. Strong. Almost frightening with the dark stubble along his jaw, his glistening muscles. So *male*.

He could have posed for one of those underwear ads. He was the kind of guy women panted over.

She couldn't believe she'd done what she had done. With *him*.

"You turned off the light," he said.

"The moon is back." For now, it was better this way. She could only be so bold, so brazen.

His hand moved across her belly, then his knuckles skimmed the triangle of hair between her thighs, where already she felt wet for him again.

"Did you like it?" he asked, his voice deep and husky.

She thought about the way he'd filled her. "Yes." Her voice was a drifting leaf, anticipating his next move, wanting it.

"Everything?"

"Everything."

"What did you like best?"

This was so personal. She was glad he couldn't see the heat in her face. She swallowed. "Feeling you inside me."

She heard his quick intake of breath. She could feel his heart pounding against hers.

She took a chance. Squeezing her eyes shut, she asked, "And you? Did you like it at all?"

"Lark. Sweet, sweet Lark. I loved it. You are the sweetest, hottest, most erotic woman . . ."

To demonstrate just how much he'd liked he, he began kissing her. All over. He slowly worked his way down her melting body.

Down.

Down.

His mouth was on her belly. His hair brushed her abdomen.

Down.

Down.

And then she felt the abrasive roughness of his beard on her inner thighs, felt his strong hands cupping her buttocks, lifting her to his mouth.

She felt a brief moment of panic. "Nathan, I don't know—"

"Trust me, Lark. I'll take care of you."

His tongue was hot and wet and knowing. She was powerless. She was under his control.

She let go. And spasmed against him again and again, to finally lie limp and spent.

She thought he was done when she heard a now familiar sound. A package being opened.

And then he was between her thighs, whispering encouragements as he slid inside her, awakening her again until she was with him, meeting him thrust for thrust, cry for cry.

Lark had almost drifted off to sleep, this time with Nathan's arm around her, her head against his chest, when his voice came out of the darkness, startling her awake.

"I'd like to kill that bastard."

"Who?" What was he talking about? The violence in his voice scared her.

"The guy who hurt you."

She didn't like hearing him talk about killing someone. "He's already dead."

"Yeah? Good."

"He went to prison, but then he got out for good behavior." She laughed, unable to hide her bitterness. "I was scared to death. Scared he'd come looking for me. And then, not two weeks after he'd gotten out, he crashed his car into a cement wall and was killed. He was dead, but his death didn't undo what had happened. It was something I had to deal with, something I had to get past."

"It would have given me extreme satisfaction to work him over."

Nathan's words sent a new kind of chill through her, brought up something she kept losing track of in her infatuation for this man. The fact that Nathan Senatra might be a murderer.

20

The slam of a car door disturbed Lark somewhere deep in the recesses of sleep.

Then came voices.

Low. Male.

Drifting to Lark from far away.

She came awake with a start, grounded yet still groggy, still confused.

It was morning.

She was in Nathan's room. In Nathan's bed.

Alone.

Naked.

And there were people outside.

This time she didn't lie there hoping her clothes would magically fall into place. This time, careful to keep a low profile, she scrambled into her things.

Her clothes were impossibly wrinkled and limp, the high humidity having saturated the fabric, making it take on a strange quality all its own. Her skin itself felt moist. Her hair clung to her arms.

She hurried to the window. Standing to one side, she peeked out.

A police car.

Adam Trent.

He stood in the overgrown yard, his uniform looking a little limp too. Beside him was another officer—the young man who'd pulled her over that first day. What was his name? Harris. Officer Harris.

Trent's voice carried up to her. "Ever seen these before?"

In his hand was rubber tubing with capped ends. Spark plug wires.

From her position at the window, she couldn't see Nathan. When he answered, his voice was a deep rumble, too low to make out any words.

"These particular wires happen to be exactly like the ones taken from Miss Leopold's car two days ago."

Lark's breath caught.

"In fact, I would venture to say these *are* the wires taken from Miss Leopold's car."

If Nathan replied, Lark didn't hear it.

Trent continued. "Someone called us with an anonymous tip." He paused for effect. "We found these under the seat of your truck."

Lark put a hand to her mouth and pulled back from the window. *Not Nathan. It couldn't have been Nathan.*

From down below came a shout. "You son of a bitch!"

Lark swung back to the window in time to see Nathan come off the steps in a flying tackle, carrying Trent to the ground. Trent recovered quickly, pulling back a fist, landing a blow that sent Nathan's head jerking back. And then it was just a tangle of arms and legs, the struggle punctuated by the sound of grunts, of knuckles making contact with flesh and bone.

Harris stood to one side, an expression of total disbelief on his face, an expression that would have been comical under any other circumstances.

At the moment, Lark felt like throwing up.

Instead, heart hammering, she shoved herself away from the window. She took a trembling step, half expecting the very floor to dissolve under her. And then she was hurrying down the stairs and through the kitchen.

Outside, the men were still locked together, cussing and muttering, trying to get new holds, appearing to have reached a stalemate.

Sunlight glinted off something in the deputy's hand—her sense of unreality deepened. Everything became disjointed. Time stopped.

A gun.

Harris had a gun.

He pressed it to Nathan's temple.

Oh God.

"That's enough!"

The nervous command came from Harris.

When she thought Nathan's behavior couldn't get any more irrational, his arm came up, knocking the gun from the officer's hand, sending the weapon flying through the air.

Harris stumbled backward.

In half a heartbeat, Nathan was scrambling after the pistol. His fingers wrapped around it. And then he was staggering to his feet, gun in hand.

Trent and Harris froze.

The scene before her became a series of freeze-framed images burned into her brain.

Nathan, shirtless, bloody, a gun in his hand. A man who, only hours ago, had held *her,* had whispered to her, soothed her, loved her.

With his free hand, Nathan wiped at the blood streaming from his nose, then put his hand to his shoulder, wincing in pain.

Slowly, never taking his eyes from Nathan, Trent got to his feet, hands dangling at his sides.

Nathan let the gun move from Harris to Trent, back to Harris, while he stood there, gasping for air.

It was like a violent, horrible movie she couldn't quit watching. A nightmare she couldn't shake.

"Nathan!"

Without conscious thought, she screamed his name, her voice ringing out in the stillness of the morning. It was a plea, not only for Nathan to put down the gun, but for him to tell her none of this was real, none of it was really happening.

The officers' heads came up. Two pairs of eyes stared at her, taking in her wild, disheveled appearance.

"Lark."

Nathan spoke without taking his eyes from the officers. "Go back in the house." His voice was quiet, controlled, at odds with the ferociousness of his appearance.

She stepped off the porch. "No."

"Lark—"

"No."

Nathan's swung around to her. *Get away,* his eyes pleaded.

Deep down, she understood that he didn't want her to witness his shame, didn't want her to see this side of him.

"Do what he says." It was Trent speaking. "Go back in the house. So you don't get hurt."

Lark suddenly felt a strange sense of calm, a feeling of power. "Nathan, put the gun down. Please."

She saw his hesitation, saw something flicker deep within his eyes.

So did Harris.

He grabbed at his belt. Then he lunged.

Nathan cried out. His body jerked.

Once. Twice. His eyes rolled back in his head and he buckled to the ground.

Without thought, Lark ran across the yard, dropping to her knees in the wet grass.

Nathan was sprawled on his back, unconscious. His face, beneath the blood, beneath the blue-black stubble of his unshaven face, was ashen.

Was he breathing? Did he have a heartbeat? Shaking fingers searched, finding a pulse in his neck.

Thank God.

A hand held above his nose and mouth detected a stir of air.

Her eyes made a frantic search of his body. She couldn't find a wound. "What did you do to him?" she demanded.

Harris slid something into his belt, something black and rectangular. "Stun gun."

Behind him, Trent picked up the weapon that had fallen from Nathan's grip.

"He should be coming around in a few seconds," Trent said.

As she watched, Nathan began to move slightly. His eyes came open. For a moment, he just lay there, looking up at the sky, the sunlight reflecting in the deep blue irises she'd once thought were the most beautiful shade of blue she'd ever seen. Then, as if sensing her presence, he turned his head, his eyes searching, finding her.

"Lark."

His tone held intimacy.

Nathan lifted a hand to her, a sweet, groggy, imploring gesture.

I'll take care of you, he'd told her. When had he spoken those words? Just hours ago? It seemed like it had happened in another life.

Someone grabbed her and pulled her to her feet. She looked up. Trent. One eye was swollen. So was his bottom lip.

Good, she thought, wondering if she was completely insane.

His shirt was bloodstained, most of the blood Nathan's. Trent had definitely come out the victor. He'd kept his head, while Nathan had just reacted.

"Stay away from him," Trent said, keeping a firm grip on her arm.

"He's not going to do anything," she said. "He doesn't even know where he is."

She looked back.

Nathan's hand was still extended to her.

"Commere," he said. "Havta tell you … tell you … somethin'."

But Trent wouldn't loosen his hold on her. "He might not be as out of it as he seems."

With Nathan's eyes still on hers, she moved away.

She watched as the officers rolled him to his stomach, watched as they pulled his hands behind his back, heard his cry of pain.

"Don't hurt him!"

The handcuffs snapped into place.

"You are under arrest for assaulting an officer," Trent said, sounding satisfied. "And for suspicion of the murder of Mary Jane Senatra. Read him his rights."

Lark continued to back away. She wanted to cover her ears, cover her eyes. Deny it all. She bumped up against the porch railing. Her hand fumbled, grabbing the wood for support. She lowered herself, leg shaking.

She watched as, arms pinned behind him, Nathan was dragged to his feet. Once upright, he stood there swaying, looking pale and weak, as if he might pass out.

They walked him to the car. His gait was unsure, stumbling. Harris opened the back door.

Before getting inside, Nathan's head came up. His gaze moved across the expanse of yard . . . until he found her.

He stared for what seemed like minutes. She could almost read his thoughts, see as he struggled to make sense of the senseless, fought for words to explain the unexplainable.

"Get the hell out of here."

His voice was wooden. Dead.

Trent shoved at the top of Nathan's head, pushing him into the backseat. The door slammed behind him.

Lark wanted to be alone. Had to be alone.

Instead of getting into the driver's seat, Trent turned around and crossed the yard to stand in front of her.

With his black eye and swollen lip, he was even more intimidating than usual. "I'm sorry you had to witness this," he said.

He braced a hand against the porch railing and leaned closer. "Did he hurt you?"

Hurt her?

She looked toward the squad car. She could see Nathan inside the caged backseat, sitting there, staring straight ahead.

She didn't know what to think. She didn't believe he'd tampered with her car, yet he'd pulled a gun on a cop. What kind of person did that?

"He didn't hurt me."

"He's a hothead. He has no respect for women. Are you sure he didn't hit you? Or force you to do anything you didn't want to do? Anything you might want to press charges for?"

"No."

"Sometimes people don't want to admit to things because they're scared. That's understandable. But we're close to pinning this murder on him. All we need are the DNA results and we'll have him. When that happens, he'll be put away for a long time."

No. This wasn't happening.

"You'll be safe. You won't have anything to be afraid of."

"He didn't hurt me."

"Sometimes women think they can redeem a guy like Senatra. Truth is, nobody can fix them. You're only fooling yourself if you think you can." He exhaled and shoved the hair back from his forehead. "I think maybe you should do what Senatra suggested. It would probably be a good time for you to go home, to get out of here."

"Are you telling me to get out of town, Officer Trent?"

He stared at her with his dark, cold eyes. "Yes."

With that, he turned and left, taking Nathan with him.

She didn't watch the car pull away. Instead, feeling very, very old, she turned and walked up the steps, into the house.

Could she have been wrong about Nathan? Was it like Trent had said? Had she thought she could save him? Change him? Or had she simply created him? Nathan Senatra. Taken a man and given him the traits she wanted him to have? Had he simply been a product of her own need?

No.

But he pulled a gun on a policeman.

Once inside the kitchen, she let her gaze track numbly around the room.

He'd been out feeding the calf. The bottle was next to the sink, freshly rinsed. Next to that, tucked into a clear jar, the kind used for canning fruits or vegetables, was a bouquet of tiny, delicate violets.

$\overline{21}$

Everytime the squad car hit a pothole, the pain in Nathan's shoulder went from intense to blinding. But even that wasn't enough to block out the memory of Lark's scream. And her horrified expression when he'd looked up at her, gun in hand.

In that blackest of moments, now indelibly in-grained into his memory, he'd wondered how the hell life had become so ugly. He'd felt the warm weight of the gun in his hand, and wondered how the hell it had gotten there. Had he lost his damn mind?

Maybe.

Probably.

At some point in the confrontation, his brain had shut down and he'd switched to pure reaction, pure survival instinct.

When somebody shoves a gun in your face, you get it out of there, fast. It had been reflex, nothing more.

But picking up the gun after Harris had dropped it, now that was another thing altogether.

He'd been cornered. Trapped. His instinct had been to back them off enough for him to get away.

But then Lark had called his name. *Screamed* his name.

The horror, the fear he'd seen in her face had shaken him enough to make him take a mental step back, enough to look at himself, see what he was doing.

Christ.

For a minute, it had seemed like the old days. Just two guys hashing it out, going at it, beating the crap out of each other.

For one insane minute, he'd forgotten about the badge.

But the gun . . . the gun. Jeez. He didn't like guns. He didn't even own a gun. As a kid, he'd only been hunting once. Just once. When he'd gotten that coyote in his sights, he couldn't pull the trigger. No way could he do it.

Lark.

Why'd she have to witness his shame?

He thought about standing there in front of her, hands bound, shirtless, not even able to wipe the blood from his own face. At that moment, he'd thought, I've fallen as far as a man can fall.

And he'd decided that he probably *had* killed Mary Jane, even if he couldn't remember doing it.

They hit another bump. A big one.

A red-hot poker of pain shot up his arm, across his collarbone. For a second he thought he was going to pass out. He squeezed his eyes shut, tipped back his head, and tried to breathe shallowly.

Lark.

God, Lark.

His one real regret in this whole awful mess was dragging Lark into it, dragging her down with him.

She would go home. She would go back to where she belonged. And maybe, with time, she would forget.

He was kidding himself. She wouldn't forget. And she would never trust another man. He'd screwed up her life for good.

When he'd come to there on the ground, he'd thought the whole thing with Trent had been a dream, a nightmare. In his dazed state, he'd almost told Lark he loved her.

They hit another bump. A big one. Nathan bit his lip to keep from crying out. He felt a sheen of sweat break out on his body. Behind his eyelids, he saw a swirling red, a red that pulsated with every beat of his heart.

Another bump.

Everything turned black and he slumped down in the seat.

"I think he's faking it."

Harris.

His voice came to Nathan through a haze of pain.

"Come on, Senatra."

Trent.

"We're home. Out of the car."

Nathan tried to lift his foot, but it had a boot attached to it. A boot that was so heavy he couldn't lift it. Helluva deal.

Somebody grabbed his arm, which was already twisted behind his back. They lifted and pulled, the movement grinding splintered bone against splintered bone. His feet tangled under him like some damn puppet's. Through a tidal wave roar in his head, he caught a glimpse of Trent's face, felt hands on him as he buckled, then heard Trent's voice say, "He ain't fakin'."

Doc Bailey.

Why'd they have to go and call Doc Bailey to witness his humiliation, his total fall from grace? Doc Bailey had delivered him.

"How many times you broke that collarbone now?" Doc asked as he finished wrapping the white bandage around Nathan's right pectoral, collarbone, and chest.

Nathan closed his eyes and rested his head against the cement block wall of the jail cell. "Three, I think," he mumbled.

"Let's see. There was that time you got bucked off a horse. And that time you were trying to get a newborn calf to suck and the mother came at you. Got a few ribs along with that, if I recall."

"You recall."

"That should do it. I'll leave some pain pills with Adam."

Nathan opened his eyes a crack. Doc Bailey was looking around the cell, taking in the pornography on the graffiti-covered walls. "Never thought I'd be working on you here." He sighed. "I've delivered a lot of babies to all sorts of families. You were one of my first. I was young. Scared, to tell the truth. Naive. I thought each baby was a miracle, a gift—which they are. It just never entered my head, the day I delivered you, that I might be delivering a criminal."

He snapped the case shut. "My wife's been nagging me to take early retirement." He sighed and turned to the door, calling for the guard. "I think I will." He spoke to himself, his shoulders sagging with the weight of his burden. "I think I will."

Another stain on Nathan's already overcrowded soul.

An hour later, after the pain pill Doc Bailey left kicked in, Nathan began to worry. He had to do something about the cattle. The bottle calf would be hungry, bawling its head off about now.

And what about Lark? Was she on the road, driving home? Would she be able to concentrate on the driving with all that had happened?

Those damn spark plug wires. Found in his truck. A lie. A damn lie. He may have forgotten what had happened the night of Mary Jane's murder, but he sure as hell knew he'd never taken any spark plug wires from Lark's car.

He'd just assumed Trent had been lying, making up the whole thing. Trent had wanted to get Nathan behind bars ever since Mary Jane's death. *Before* Mary Jane's death. Nathan had just figured the son of a bitch was trying to frame him. But now that he thought about it, now that his rage wasn't overriding his reason, there was another possibility. Maybe someone else had planted them in his truck. For Trent to find.

It didn't take Lark long to find the jail, which was located across the street and down an alley from the police station. In a town the size of Elizabeth, finding anything was easy.

Before she chickened out, Lark parked, walked up the wide sidewalk to the front desk, and asked to see Nathan.

"Down the hall." Without looking up, the woman pointed over her shoulder. "Last cell on the left."

"Don't I need to go through some kind of security or something?"

The woman stopped pushing her papers long enough to present Lark with a bored expression. "Honey, this is Metamora County, not L.A."

Lark walked down the narrow hall. At the end was a dimly lit cell. She could just make out the shape of a person lying on a cot. Beside the cot was a sink. And a stainless steel toilet. Absolutely no privacy.

Unbidden, Nathan's words came back to her. *Not exactly five-star accommodations.*

Hearing footsteps, Nathan swung his legs to the side of the cot and looked up.

"Lark?"

His voice came to her out of the dingy darkness. He sounded surprised to see her. And puzzled. Ashamed.

He got to his feet, his movements stiff. And when he stood up, she saw the bandage around his arm and across his chest. Following the direction of his gaze, he waved a hand at the white cloth. "Broke a collarbone."

He came close enough to wrap his fingers around the cell bars.

Just another image for her to take away with her, another Metamora County souvenir.

He looked awful, or at least as awful as Nathan Senatra could look. His face had been cleaned up, but he needed to shave and there was a butterfly bandage across one brow, along with deep bruises under his eyes. It looked as if he hadn't slept in a week.

"What are you doing here?"

She'd come for answers, but now, seeing him face to face, her resolve weakened. She hedged. "I didn't come to break you out, if that's what you're hoping."

He started to laugh, but ended up gasping, a hand to his shoulder.

"I couldn't just leave with no one to take care of the cattle. What are you going to do about them?"

"Trent's working on that. I told him I'd have the Humane Society on his ass if he didn't get somebody out there soon."

"What about right now? What about the calf? I couldn't find any milk."

Nathan dropped his hand back to the bar. "There isn't any. I was going to pick up a bag today."

She had to leave. She couldn't take it anymore, couldn't go through with the questions she'd come to ask. This was the man who barely hours ago had held her so tenderly, who had calmed her fears, who had stolen a little bit of her soul.

"I'll get some milk replacer," she said. "I'll feed the calf."

Then, before she broke down, she turned and hurried away.

Nathan stood there, his forehead against the cool metal bars.

He closed his eyes.

He tried to ignore the pain that had lodged in his throat.

A few minutes later, he heard a sound. Slowly, he lifted his head.

She was back.

Standing there, hands clasped together the way she'd done before they'd made love.

In that instant, his heart broke.

"Was any of it real?" she asked. Her voice was thick.

When he looked closer, he could see that her eyes were red. He could still taste her, still smell the scent of her, as if she'd permeated his skin.

"Was any of it real? Any of what you said? Any of what we did? Are you even who I think you are? Or are you someone I made up?"

He'd hurt her.

He'd never meant to hurt her.

"I keep asking myself, What am I supposed to think? There you were, with a gun in your hand, holding it on a cop. What kind of person does that?"

She was right.

"But you know what?"

Her voice was teary, tremulous. It had taken a lot of guts for her to come and face him after all that had happened.

"What?"

She was looking directly into his eyes. Suddenly he sensed a strength about her, a resolve.

"You may have taken Harris's gun, but you didn't take the wires from my car. And you didn't kill Mary Jane."

He couldn't have heard right. "W-what?"

"You asked me if I ever believed in anything without question." She paused for a heartbeat. "You, I believe in you."

"I was talking about believing the world is round even when it looks flat. I was talking about believing that astronauts really walked on the moon." He'd hurt her. If she stuck around, he'd hurt her again. *She* might believe he didn't kill Mary Jane, but Nathan wasn't too sure. Not sure at all. "If you're smart, you'll go home. You'll get away from here as fast as you can. I'm bad news."

She smiled. A sweet, tender smile. "I know." She touched his cheek. "But I'm staying anyway."

And then she left.

When she was gone, he pushed himself away from the bars and staggered backwards, finding the cot, collapsing there, unsuccessfully trying to absorb what had just happened.

How could she believe in him, when he didn't even believe in himself?

22

When Lark stepped inside the feed store, all conversation ceased. About a dozen farmers, seeking out air-conditioning, darkness, and the comfort of their own kind, sat in metal folding chairs lined up along opposite walls. Every one of them sported a different brand of seed-corn cap, the kind with the snap back that was supposed to be one size fits all, but instead was one size fits nobody.

There was no doubt as to the topic of their conversation. It wasn't everyday one of their native sons was arrested for murder. They were probably agreeing that it couldn't have happened to a nicer, more deserving guy.

Approaching the counter was like walking the gauntlet. Without looking left or right, Lark could feel every eye in the place on her.

She told the man behind the counter what she needed.

"Nathan Senatra no longer has an account here."

She could sense the collective, rapt interest of the room.

"I'll pay cash for it."

Behind her came much shuffling of feet and coughing.

She paid, then waited until the man at the counter returned with a bag over one shoulder.

"Want me to load it for you?" he asked, waiting.

"Don't bother."

Expressionless, he slid the bag across the counter—while she prayed it wasn't too terribly heavy.

It wasn't.

Twenty pounds at the most. She lifted it. Then, carrying it in her arms like a baby, she left.

What a relief to step outside into the stifling Midwestern heat and blinding sun.

She dropped the bag of dry milk into her trunk and brushed the fine white dust from her palms.

Someone shouted her name.

She looked up to see Brett getting out of his car, hurrying toward her.

"Lark! Hi."

She'd hoped to get in and out of town without running into anybody she knew, not that she knew many people in Elizabeth. It was just that small talk was the last thing she felt like engaging in at the moment.

Brett looked in her trunk and spotted the dry milk. "Let me guess. You're on some kind of special diet."

She wasn't in the mood for jokes. "Brett, I have to get going." She slammed the lid, rounded the car, and slid into the driver's seat. Before she could shut the door, Brett wedged himself in the opening, one hand braced on the door, the other on the car roof.

She turned the ignition key, hoping he'd get the hint. "I have to feed a calf."

"Nathan's? I heard he was in jail."

"Yes."

Something flickered in his eyes, then it was gone. "So, would you like to go out again some time?"

She didn't want to hurt his feelings, but she was too emotionally drained to come up with a soft response. She couldn't come up with any response.

"Guess that's a no, huh?"

"Brett, I—"

"That night we went to the drive-in. Did you have a good time?"

He watched her closely.

"I had a great time." It was true. But that was before Nathan.

He nodded, his expression preoccupied. Then he said something she didn't catch.

"What?" She was thinking about Nathan. About needing to get a lawyer. A bondsman. Whatever it took to get him out of jail.

"Maybe I'll stop by Nathan's when I get off work. Will you be there?"

"Yes, but I'll be busy."

"Yeah. Sure. Okay."

He backed away. She shut the door, gave him a wave, and drove off.

It had been hot for so many days that Nathan's house had absorbed and stored the heat. Even though the windows were open, it was at least fifteen degrees hotter inside than out.

The flowers were still next to the sink, looking as if

they'd just been picked. And even though the farmhouse seemed abandoned, as if someone had never finished moving in, she could feel Nathan's presence.

She followed the mixing instructions on the bag of powdered milk, then headed out to the pasture to feed the calf.

She heard him before she saw him. And when she got there, he almost knocked her down trying to get to the bottle. It took him less than thirty seconds to polish off the whole two quarts. When the bottle was empty, he butted her, bawling, wanting more.

She tried to pet him, reassure him, but he wasn't the least bit interested in the feel of her hand. He tossed his head, made an angry sound deep in his throat, his only interest being in what she no longer had.

"Mothers are never appreciated," she told the ungrateful guy.

He continued to butt her, rubbing his wet muzzle against the hem of her jean shorts, getting the fabric damp.

She checked the calf feeders. There was still a lot of grain in them. The cows didn't seem to be in any distress. Some were lying in groups. Others stood, chewing their cud. Still others munched at the grass.

Content.

At least somebody was.

She left, stepping over the electric fence, careful to avoid the wire.

She kept thinking about how Nathan had looked in jail.

Beaten.

Defeated.

He couldn't stay there.

On the way back to the house, she felt light-headed

and realized she hadn't eaten anything all day. But the thought of food turned her stomach.

Reaching the shade of the porch, she put down the empty bottle and sank into the green wicker rocker. With the intention of fanning her face, she picked up a magazine from a stack on the floor, the title catching her eye.

Terra Firma.

Her mind went back to that first day when she'd raced to the gas station to use the phone. One of the men had talked about how Nathan was involved in some environmental publication. *Terra Firma.* That's what he'd called it.

The magazine was made of rough paper, most likely recycled, the print had an odor, most likely made from soybeans. It was basically a collection of how-to articles put together by various farmers, kind of what-worked-for-me stuff. There was an article on organic farming. Another on the humane treatment of animals. One on planting, not only crops, but trees. Crop rotation. Windbreaks. Wildlife strips.

It all sounded sensible, practical, environmentally conscious. But, from what she'd gathered, such thinking wasn't the norm.

Nathan Senatra had been swimming against the current all his life.

She thumbed through it again. This time she noticed that an article on the very last page had been written by Nathan. In it, he told about how he was working to develop a hybrid sunflower, a double-dwarf, one that could better tolerate heat and moisture, plus produce higher yields. It told about how he grew the special seeds in flats in an upstairs bedroom of his house.

Oh my God.

She read on.

It had taken him years to reach that point, but soon he hoped to have the perfect plant.

My God.

The seeds.

She hadn't thrown out his marijuana, she'd destroyed years of work. He'd had every right to be furious with her.

And yet, he'd come back and apologized.

She was so lost in her own misery, so lost in thought, that she didn't hear the car until it pulled to a stop.

A police car.

Adam Trent stepped out. It was the first time she'd seen him in civilian clothes. He was dressed in jeans, cowboy boots, and a sleeveless chambray shirt. The muscles in his arms were massive.

All along, she'd thought the uniform had been part of the intimidation. Not so. For some reason, the everyday clothes made him seem all the more dangerous.

He made a quick perusal of the area, then his eyes came back to her. He gave her a nod, then crossed the yard to the porch, one foot propped on the top step, a hand on the railing.

He was so stern. Did he ever laugh out loud? She couldn't imagine it. He would never allow himself to lose control to that extent.

"I had the feeling you might still be around."

She ignored his comment. "Has Nathan's bond been set?" She didn't know much about such things, but she knew Nathan couldn't get out of jail until his bond was paid.

"No, and it won't be for three more days."

Three days. She hated to think of him stuck there for three more days.

"And since this is also a murder case, the judge might not set bail at all."

No bail? Could they do that?

Blackbirds called from a nearby evergreen. It surprised Lark to see that the sky was getting dark.

Earlier, she'd told Nathan she hadn't come to break him out. Now the idea didn't seem so far-fetched.

They didn't watch him very closely.

She could sneak him past the front desk. Then they would—

"You can't stay here," Trent said, interrupting her bold musings.

She started rocking, hoping for the illusion of tranquillity. "I don't have much choice. I've been thrown out of the only bed and breakfast in town."

"Mrs. B runs a tight ship."

"A narrow-minded ship."

"This isn't Hollywood or wherever you're from. If you don't want to draw attention to yourself, you have to behave. Small towns play by a whole different set of rules. They aren't as morally lax as other places. Some things just aren't acceptable."

She stopped rocking. "Just because someone is from California doesn't mean she subscribes to a promiscuous lifestyle."

"Look," he said, "I know you think I'm being hardnosed about this, but there's a possibility we might have to seal off the house."

They wouldn't seal off a house weeks after the murder, would they? That didn't make sense. "I have nowhere else to go."

"Come to my place. You'll be safe there."

She stared, dumbfounded.

He looked down at the railing, rubbing his thumb

along the grain of the wood. "I haven't been with a woman in a long time." He looked back up. The hungry animal sensuality in his eyes jolted her.

"I'll fix you supper. Steak. Do you like steak?" Then, "I'd make it worth your while."

The last sentence brought her around. She jumped to her feet, hands clenched. "I think you'd better leave."

He drew back. Anger flashed in the depths of his eyes.

She'd made him mad. Oh Lord. Panic beat like small wings in her chest.

The farm was so isolated. So far from anybody. Trent could do anything he wanted with her.

He could rape her.

He could kill her.

Throw her in the pond.

Her mind raced.

It was strange how Trent had just shown up the day her car had been vandalized. How he'd just found her by the road that morning. How he'd almost talked her into leaving in his squad car, but then Brett had happened along and she'd gotten a ride with him instead.

Had Trent taken the wires from her car, put the same ones back in, then used another set to implicate Nathan?

She had another horrifying thought: If Nathan couldn't remember what had happened the night Mary Jane was murdered, then he was the perfect person to frame.

"You have something against cops?" Trent asked, drawing her back to the present, drawing her back to his anger, which was still quite apparent.

"No." Stall. Try not to make him any angrier. "I'm not sure what you're suggesting, but if it's what I think, well,

I'm not that kind of girl." A harmless enough line, she hoped.

He tried to smile, but couldn't. His face just wouldn't do it. What he came up with was something feral.

Goose bumps ran up the back of her neck.

"You've done Senatra, but you won't do me?"

This was insane. Until last night, she'd never really had sex in her whole life, and here he was thinking she was some kind of hooker.

"It could be good. I'd make sure of it."

Looking at him, she could believe that. But not with her. She found his desire terrifying.

"Do you have some misplaced notion about being loyal to Senatra?" Trent let out a bitter snort. "The guy has no respect for women. He uses them up and spits them out. Fifteen years ago, he got my sister pregnant, then dumped her."

Lark gasped. His sister? Pregnant? With Nathan's baby? She'd thought nothing else could shock her. She was wrong.

"You know what my sister did?"

Lark slowly shook her head, trying to absorb this new information, trying to sort out lie from truth.

"She tried to kill herself."

Lark didn't want to hear any more, but Trent kept talking.

"Over Senatra. She lived, but she ended up losing the baby."

"How horrible." Horrible, horrible, horrible.

"Since then, she's been in and out of mental institutions."

"I-I'm sorry."

Everything fell into place. The motive. There it was. Revenge.

"I'm sorry too."

Trent had murdered Mary Jane and was using her death to frame Nathan.

"Forget Senatra. He's poison." Trent stared at her, then asked, "So, are you coming?"

She looked at the roped muscles in his arms. She thought about the number he'd done on Nathan that morning. Nathan was strong, tough, yet Trent had come away with hardly a scratch. Now, towering over her, he scared her to death. Fear beat through her as she slowly shook her head from side to side.

She held her breath and watched in horror as he struggled with his anger, got it under control. "I'm not the kind of guy to force myself on a woman," he said. "But I'll be back. To make sure you're gone."

He was leaving. Thank God. Oh, thank God.

Lark stood on the porch and watched him go, watched as his taillights faded in the distance, watched until the last of the dust had settled. She ran inside, slammed and locked the door, then collapsed against it, her palms pressed to the hot, sticky wood, eyes closed.

Trent was the murderer.

What was she going to do?

Call the police?

She laughed—a pathetically hollow sound. He *was* the police.

Nathan didn't have a phone. She would have to leave the house. She would have to go to the gas station, the one she'd gone to that first day. She would tell somebody. Call somebody.

Suddenly, right behind her head, came a knock.

She screamed.

"Lark!"

From the other side of the locked door, came Brett's voice.

He knocked again.

"Brett!"

Quickly, she unlocked the door, opening it wide.

Brett stood on the porch looking safe and familiar.

She'd never been so glad to see anybody in her life.

"Brett!" She grabbed him by the arm, pulled him inside, and locked the door behind him. She tried to tell him everything at once, her words tumbling from her, one on top of the other.

$\overline{23}$

"I think Adam Trent killed Mary Jane."

Brett grabbed Lark by both arms. "Slow down. Slow down!"

She took a gulp of air. "Trent was just here," she explained, her words coming out in a rush. "He said some strange things."

"He didn't hurt you, did he?"

Brett's concern was touching. She didn't realize how alone she'd felt until that moment. "No. He didn't hurt me." She thought about the look in Trent's eyes, the way he'd promised to be back. "But he scared me," she admitted.

"What'd he say? What'd he do?"

She caught a whiff of alcohol. Brett had been drinking, she realized, her heart sinking. Was he in any shape to help? "He was talking about his sister."

Brett's hands fell away. "Nancy?"

Unconsciously, Lark rubbed her arms. "I don't think

he mentioned her name." She began to pace. "He told me how she'd been pregnant with Nathan's baby. About how she'd tried to kill herself."

Brett didn't say anything.

She stopped and looked up, arrested by the oddness of his expression. His mouth was open, his gaze far away.

"Did you know her?" she asked. "His sister?"

Her question coaxed him back.

"Yeah." His eyes were more direct, but his voice was still vague. He wasn't completely with her. "You could say that. She was a couple of years ahead of me at school."

He swayed, caught himself, then straightened.

"You've been drinking."

Quite a lot, she now realized, dismayed and irritated at the same time.

"So? Not much else to do around this place."

His answer surprised her. "I thought you liked it here."

"Like it? I *loathe* it! We're talking Iowa, for Chrissake!"

That's not what he'd told her when they'd first met. Was it the alcohol talking, or was he really so dissatisfied with his life? "Then why stay?" He was single. He had nothing holding him there.

"Don't you get it? This is the place losers go."

What was he talking about? She shook her head. "You aren't a loser."

He let out a sarcastic laugh. "You don't know anything about me. And that's fine with you. You don't *want* to know anything about me, isn't that right?"

"No."

But his words held some truth. She thought of her

impatience with him earlier in the day and realized she hadn't been a friend to him, not in the way he'd been one to her.

"Did you know that I was going to teach at the university? You didn't, did you? But when I had to get up in front of people, I froze. I couldn't do it. How can a teacher be a teacher if he can't get up in front of people? So I ran away. I came back here to hide."

"There are ways to get over that kind of fear."

"Don't you think I tried them? I tried them all. Hypnosis. Drugs. Drinking. Nothing worked."

He waved his hand. "Doesn't matter. I found out I belong here. I found out it's impossible to leave a place where you've been miserable. Harder to do than leaving a place where you've been happy. Ever notice that?" He didn't wait for an answer. "There are too many pieces of my soul here. To leave made me a nobody, a form with no substance. *That's* why I couldn't stand up in front of those people. *I wasn't really there*. Don't you see? I'd left my essence here, in Metamora County."

The squad car's headlights cut through the darkness, the cruise control set at exactly fifty-five.

Adam Trent had actually found himself attracted to Lark Leopold, especially at first. She'd seemed old-fashioned. Pure, really. And there wasn't a lot of pure left in the world. He'd liked that about her. But then Brett had told him how hot she was, how they'd really steamed up his car at the drive-in. And then she'd slept with Senatra.

Senatra.

What was wrong with these women? Couldn't they see him for what he was?

At first, Adam had been disappointed to discover that

she wasn't what she seemed. But then he'd accepted it. He was used to that kind of thing. The ugly side of life. And what was wrong with two consenting adults having a good time?

The more he thought about it, the more he'd been able to visualize her pale thighs wrapped around him. The more he thought he may as well get in the game.

He'd been telling the truth when he said he hadn't been with a woman in a long time. And after hearing about Lark, he thought she'd be safe. A one-nighter was what he needed. He just hadn't expected her to turn him down.

Adam swung by the station before going home. One last check on Senatra, just to make sure he was still under lock and key. The guy could charm his way out of a maximum security prison.

He was still there, just where he was supposed to be.

The son of a bitch looked like hell. For a brief moment, Adam found himself almost feeling sorry for him. Bad idea. When you began to feel pity, when you began to think of them as human, that's when they got you.

"Still on hunger strike?" he asked.

Senatra lifted his head. His eyes were dark hollow pits. They'd given him a battery-operated razor, but he hadn't used it.

"Go to hell." His words were tough, but his voice held a deep, world-weariness. The man's life had finally caught up with him.

"Sorry about your collarbone."

"Don't worry. I normally don't believe in lawsuits, but I think one might be in order here."

"*You* came after *me*, remember?"

"I happen to take exception to being framed."

What a hardhead. "I thought maybe you were ready for a confession."

Senatra let out a derisive snort.

"Heard your grandmother came by to see you today." No answer.

"What I'll bet you don't know is that after her little visit, she dropped by my office."

That got his interest. "What would she want to see you for?"

"To reminisce. You probably don't remember, but she taught my Sunday School class. We talked about the good ol' days. But that wasn't the reason she stopped."

"Get to the point."

"Said she had a confession to make."

"What the hell are you talking about."

Adam had been saving this, savoring the anticipation of Senatra's reaction. "She confessed to killing your ex-wife."

Senatra didn't disappoint him. In a fraction of a second, he was on his feet. He flew to the bars. "You son of a bitch! You're lying. You're a lying bastard."

"Think so?" Adam pulled a micro-cassette recorder from his shirt pocket, held it up for Senatra to see, then pushed the PLAY button.

Over the tiny speaker came the recorded voice of Millie Senatra, sweetly explaining how she'd murdered poor Mary Jane.

Adam switched off the recorder and looked at Nathan, eyebrows raised in expectation.

Rage.

That was the only word that would come close to Senatra's reaction. He was bare teeth and stretched tendons. He rattled the cell bars, then reached his arm through as far as he could. Adam jumped back, managing to stay just beyond Senatra's clenched fingers.

Millie was a sweetheart. She'd tried to save her grandson. It was as simple as that. The poor woman hadn't known she'd been playing right into Adam's hands. Senatra might be a criminal, but everybody knew he doted on his grandmother. He wouldn't let her go to jail for him.

"What about it?" Adam asked, holding up the recorder. "You ready to make *your* confession?"

Senatra let out a furious roar and gave the bars another frustrated shake.

It was a good feeling, seeing Senatra squirm. So good, Adam couldn't resist one final dig. "You know the woman from California?"

Senatra stopped rattling his cage and listened with the intensity of a wild animal.

Adam thought about the way he'd hoped it would have been with Lark. "She's a lot hotter than she looks." Sometimes it took a lie to get to the truth.

"What are you talking about? Did you touch her? If you touched her, I'll kill you. I swear, I'll kill you."

"You really aren't in any position to do much of anything. But now, if you confess . . ."

"What about Lark?"

Adam had wanted to hurt Senatra for a long, long time. But now, when he was about to twist the knife, he hesitated, wondering if he'd become one of them. Wondering if he'd become just as inhuman as the people he'd sworn to put behind bars.

"Tell me the truth, you asshole," came the sweet words Trent had been waiting weeks to hear. "Tell me the truth and I'll confess. I'll come clean about the night Mary Jane died."

∘   ∘   ∘

"I think you'd better go."

Lark stood with her back to the sink, her arms crossed at her waist, watching Brett.

He ignored her request. Instead of leaving, he opened the refrigerator, slid some things around on the metal rack, then straightened up, a beer in his hand. He popped the top, then settled himself in a chair, propping his brown leather loafers on the kitchen table.

Lark grabbed the beer from his limp fingers and shoved his feet to the floor. "You're not staying any longer."

"I thought you liked me." He looked like a pouty little boy.

"Not in this condition."

She turned to dump the beer. Before a drop spilled, he was behind her, grabbing her hand, surprising her with his strength. She struggled briefly. Realizing she wouldn't be able to win, that it was ridiculous to fight over a can of beer, she let him have it.

Cocky, he stood tall and downed the whole thing, dropped the can on the floor, smashed it with one foot, then collapsed back into the chair.

What a disgusting performance.

"You like *him*," he said out of the blue.

"Who?"

"Senatra. Just like the others. They always liked him, too."

"Is that bad?"

His feet dropped to the floor and he leaned forward. "Hell yes, it's bad. If you're me."

He was jealous of Nathan.

"Did you sleep with him?"

The directness of his question took her back. "That's none of your business."

"You did. I can tell."

"I don't believe this. Get out. Just get out." She went to the door, unlocked it, jerked it open, then stood with her hand on the knob, waiting for him to leave.

"It was always like that," he said conversationally, making no move to get up. "In school, if I liked a girl, she always liked Senatra. Girls drooled over him. Except for one. Nancy. Nancy Trent. She liked *me*."

Lark's hand fell away from the knob. "You dated Nancy Trent?"

Brett nodded, his eyes glazed, his expression far away. Then he shook his head, as if he couldn't quite believe what he was seeing. "Turned out, she was just using me to get to Senatra. You know what else? She was pregnant. But the baby wasn't Senatra's. It was mine."

Lark gasped.

He pounded his chest. "*My baby*. But she told everybody it was Senatra's. She thought if she made it public, he'd marry her. But it didn't work. Senatra just laughed at her. *He laughed*."

Lark hoped he was done. She didn't want to hear any more.

But he was on a roll.

"She tried to kill herself. Slit her wrists. Trent found her. Carried her to the hospital. She didn't die, but she lost our baby. My baby."

Oh God. How awful. What an awful, heartbreaking story. Had he carried the secret with him all these years? No wonder he'd had such a hard time coping when he tried to leave Elizabeth. "Did you tell anybody? Talk to anyone?"

"What was the point? My baby was dead, and the woman I loved had betrayed me. Destroyed me. Is that the kind of thing you want to advertise? Do you want the whole community to know you've been made a fool of?"

You can't bury the past. Lark knew that as much as anybody. It was always with you. But you can try to go on.

"Brett, I'm sorry." She touched his shoulder.

He knocked her hand away. His eyes, when they looked up, were full of tears—and resentment.

Startled, she stepped back.

Seeming satisfied that he was in no immediate danger of more physical contact, he continued, as if he needed to purge himself of something he'd kept inside for too long.

Lark let him talk. Maybe it would help.

"Then Mary Jane came along. She was nice to me. She actually *saw* me. She was attracted to me."

Mary Jane? Where did she fit into this?

"She made me feel good. Made me feel like a man again." He wiped at his eyes. He sniffled. "I asked her to marry me."

"What?" Lark reached for something, anything, her fingers making contact with the metal edge of the counter.

"When I proposed, I did it right. Flowers and all. A dozen red roses." He tilted his head toward the ceiling, his expression one of pure anguish. "I asked her if she'd have my baby—" he squeezed his eyes shut, as if the memory was too painful. "And she laughed! She laughed at me!"

Adam Trent had to call for a stenographer and two witnesses. Senatra's confession had to be legal. No loopholes.

He was waiting for them to arrive when the fax machine in the corner of his office beeped, then began printing out.

The results from the DNA lab.

Lark wanted to cover her ears, to block out Brett's confession.

"I told her to stop laughing at me, but she wouldn't. She said I was a boy in a man's body. And that she'd just wanted me for sex. For entertainment. She said she'd slept with a farmer and a plumber. She slept with a lawyer and a lawn-mower repairman, but she'd never slept with a bag boy. Bag boy. That's what she called me. And then she said she'd never really gotten over Senatra. Can you believe it? There he was again. Back in my life. Screwing everything up."

Lark found herself staring directly into his eyes. The pupils reflected light in a way they shouldn't. Bright. Glittery.

"I'm going to ask you again." His words were slow and measured. "Did you sleep with Senatra?"

Brett. It had been Brett all along. Why hadn't she seen it earlier? "*You* took my spark plug wires."

He didn't even try to deny it. "I didn't want you to leave. I wanted a few more days to prove myself, to show you it could work between us. Then Trent shows up with a new set of wires. The very same day."

"And you put them in for me."

"Wasn't that a crock?"

"Justice, I'd say."

"You were sleeping there so peacefully at that roadside stop. So deeply." He smiled a sweet, evil smile that made the hairs on her arms stand up. "You almost looked dead."

She stared, frozen in fear. She was in trouble. Big trouble.

"I've seen that expression before, Mary Jane."

He was mixing the past with the present. "I'm not Mary Jane," she said through numb lips. Earlier, the house had been smotheringly hot. Now she was freezing. Her fingers were cold. Her lips. Her cheeks.

"I'm not a violent person," he said forlornly. "I've fought for animal rights. I've marched against abortion. I *love* life. But you can understand how it makes me feel, can't you? When you laugh at me? It hurts my feelings."

"I'm not laughing. I'm not Mary Jane."

"I can't stand by and watch you make a fool of yourself, watch from the sidelines as you go after Senatra again. You can understand, can't you, how I don't want to see you grovel like that."

"I'm Lark! Lark!"

"Lark?"

Lines of puzzlement appeared between his brows, then vanished. "Lark. When you came along, you were different. You didn't look like them. They both had dark hair. Suntans. But in the end, the differences didn't go any deeper than skin and hair."

Footsteps sounded in the hall, regulation soles striking tile that had been laid over fifty years ago.

Trent. Coming back for his confession, Nathan thought, not even looking up.

"We have a problem."

Ol' Trent didn't sound as cocky as usual. In fact, he sounded as if somebody had knocked the wind out of him.

"Just got the DNA results back from the lab."

Nathan straightened, then slowly got to his feet.

"That skin and blood we took from under Mary Jane's fingernails . . . they didn't match."

Nathan wasn't sure he'd heard right.

"They weren't yours."

Before he could stop himself, Nathan let out a shout. *He didn't do it! He didn't kill Mary Jane!* Then he had another thought. "If it wasn't mine, then whose was it?"

Trent shook his head. "I wish to hell I knew." Then, "There was one other thing they found out."

"What's that?"

"Mary Jane was pregnant."

24

Brett stood in the middle of the kitchen, legs braced apart, swaying slightly. "You were just using me to make Senatra jealous."

"That's not true."

He was going to kill her.

He hadn't said so, but Lark could see it, feel it. He was going to kill her just like he killed Mary Jane.

She should have been thinking of a way out. Instead, her mind was full of thoughts of Nathan. The way he'd looked that first time she'd seen him walking across the field, the wind blowing his shirt, his hair.

She thought of him bloody and handcuffed.

She thought of him locked up, behind bars.

She felt Brett's eyes on her and looked up to meet his glittering gaze. He took a step closer, his head tilted to one side.

Frozen in fear, she watched as he reached out and

brushed his knuckles down the side of her face, his expression wistful as well as calculated.

"Lark . . ." He shook his head.

All she could think of were incredibly trite lines she'd heard in some terrible made-for-TV movie.

You need help.

You're not alone.

It isn't as hopeless as it seems.

But when she spoke, those weren't the words she heard herself saying. "You killed her, didn't you? You killed Mary Jane."

He didn't even blink. "I did her a favor."

"You took a life."

He spent a few seconds thinking that one over. His words, when they came, were chillingly emotionless. "I liked playing God. It's a very satisfying feeling."

He was insane. An insanity he'd hidden well. She could just hear it on the local news.

He was quiet. Never caused any trouble. Did they ever say, The guy was nuts. I saw it the first time I laid eyes on him?

"Until you do it, you really can't appreciate how fragile life is," Brett said calmly.

He didn't seem drunk any more. In fact, he seemed sober. Frighteningly sober.

"It was so much easier than I thought it would be."

He stepped closer, his body inches from hers, his eyes hypnotic.

She stepped back, bumping against the counter.

Trapped.

He smiled sweetly, then lifted both of his hands.

"So easy," he said, wrapping his fingers around her neck, placing both thumbs at her throat. "The kiss . . . of death." He bent his head toward her, his mouth moving closer. At the same time his fingers pressed into her throat, effectively shutting off her air supply.

Her reaction involved no conscious thought. It was pure, adrenaline-driven self-preservation. She grabbed his shoulders. At the same time, her knee came up, connecting with his crotch, a maneuver she'd learned in self-defense class but had never before put into practice.

His hands fell away.

Sweet, sweet air rushed into her burning lungs.

He let out a cry of pain and doubled over.

Coughing, she sucked in lungfuls of air, turned and ran.

Through the dark house.

Up the stairs.

To the room where Nathan's greenhouse had been.

Once there, she slammed the door, her fingers frantically searching for the lock, finally coming into contact with the cold metal of a skeleton key.

A skeleton key! She'd never get it locked.

She jiggled it, the key rattling as much as her teeth. From downstairs came the sound of footsteps making contact with a hollow wood floor.

Come on. Come on.

Turn.

Turn, she pleaded with the key.

Maybe it was rusty. Maybe it was the wrong key. Maybe it didn't work at all.

Run.

Beyond the mad hammering of her heart, the raggedness of her breathing, she heard the mechanism fall into place, metal against metal. At the same time, she heard Brett charging up the stairs.

She turned and ran to the open window.

Behind her, the door shuddered as Brett threw his weight against it.

She screamed.

"You bitch! Open the door!"

Head bent, she ducked out the window. Her feet skittered across rough shingles. She lost her balance, then quickly regained it. Taking small steps, she inched her way to the edge of the slanted roof.

The ground looked so far away, but it couldn't have been more than eight or nine feet.

Behind her came the sound of banging.

She glanced over her shoulder at the dark window, then back at the ground below.

She pulled in a deep breath.

And jumped.

One second she was on the roof, the next she was crashing to the ground, one impact point after the other making firm contact.

She sprang to her feet, a sharp pain shooting up her ankle as she ran for her car.

She jerked open the door and dove in behind the steering wheel, quickly hitting the electric Lock button.

With shaking hands, she reached for the ignition.

And felt nothing but the metal circle where the key should have been.

Gone.

Her keys were gone.

She made a frantic search of her pockets, patting, digging. Then, even though she never left her keys there, she felt under the seat.

Nothing.

Through the bug-splattered windshield she saw Brett strolling across the yard.

The doors are locked, she told herself. He can't get in. Not unless he breaks a window.

She watched him, eyes wide, her terror mounting

with each ragged breath she drew, with each hollow beat of her heart.

He raised his arm. Something in his hand caught the light.

Dangling from his fingers were her car keys.

He continued his approach, his steps slow and confident, stopping just inches from the car. With nothing but glass separating them, he bent at the waist and inserted the key in the lock of the driver's door.

Had to pay attention. Had to listen.

He turned the key.

A fraction of a second later, Lark pushed the LOCK button.

He turned the key again.

She locked it again.

He laughed. "Give it up, Mary Jane."

Mary Jane. He was still calling her Mary Jane.

"All I have to do is unhook the battery."

Was he right? Was that all he had to do? But he couldn't get the hood open without opening the door. Could he?

Suddenly Lark heard a click.

Hurry! Hurry!

She pushed the button.

To her horror, she wasn't fast enough. The driver's door swung open.

Lark screamed.

Fingers brushed her bare arm. She pushed open the passenger door and dove out. She shoved herself to her feet and ran, stumbling.

Up the dirt lane, away from the house, away from the car, away from Brett, into the darkness.

She ran, blindly.

From behind her came a shout. "Mary Jane!"

She left the lane, giving it up for the tall, ungrazed grass. Wet grass blades slashed her arms. Her foot caught in a tangle of growth. She tripped, crashing to the ground. She staggered to her feet and kept running.

Her side ached. Her lungs were raw. Pain from her ankle darted up her leg.

Maybe she could lose him in the dark. Maybe she could get away—

A beam of light—a flashlight!—darted past her. Behind her, Brett called out.

She pushed herself for more speed. It wasn't there.

I'm not going to make it.

She felt a thrust from behind, the force propelling her forward. He tackled her, knocking her to the ground face-first, the impact driving the air from her lungs.

He rolled her to her back, his hands on her shoulders, pinning her to the ground, his ragged breathing filling the air. Behind them, in the background, came the sound of disturbed cows, bawling, moving in all directions.

She felt a little burst of strength. Energy fed into her limp limbs. She struggled.

Taken by surprise, Brett's grip loosened.

She scrambled away, only to be caught by her foot and dragged back.

She curled around—and bit his hand.

He screamed and let go.

She jumped to her feet. Before she could take a step, she felt a tremendous shove.

She stumbled backward. And suddenly there was nothing beneath her.

She fell through the air, hitting the ground with bone-jarring impact. Before she had a chance to get any kind of a bearing, she was tumbling downhill, her head coming in contact with something hard.

Fireworks.

Pain zigzagging behind eyelids. Then everything turned black.

"Lark? You down there?"

Brett.

Stay still. Don't make a sound.

"Lark?"

Pain knifed through her skull. She lifted a hand to her temple. Her fingers came away sticky.

"Lark! Where are you?"

He'd called her Lark, not Mary Jane.

She lay there, praying he wouldn't be able to hear her breathing, or her frantically beating heart.

Suddenly a pinpoint of light fell directly on her face, blinding her. She squinted and held up a hand to block the glare.

No good. She couldn't run anymore.

She was going to die out there, in the middle of Nathan Senatra's pasture. And Brett would probably toss her body in the pond, just the way he'd done to Mary Jane.

Tears stung her eyes.

Nathan.

She'd never see him again.

She listened as Brett worked his way down the hillside. Above her head she saw stars. Millions of stars. They brought her a sense of calm. As she lay there, she became aware of a sound.

A popping.

What was that?

Why did it seem so familiar?

Then she remembered.

The electric fence. Electricity 101. She hadn't believed Nathan that day, but she believed him now.

A ghost of a smile touched her lips. The smile turned into a grimace of pain.

Had to get up.

But it hurt to breathe. It hurt to blink. It hurt to think.

I can't. I can't move.

Do it. Don't think. Just do it.

She didn't know how she got there, but suddenly she was on her hands and knees.

Pain. Blinding, stupefying pain.

Crawl.

She crawled.

Where? Where am I going?

Just go. Just move. Toward the popping sound.

A wave of nausea swept over her. She was going to throw up. She was going to faint.

Something ran in her eyes, blinding her. Something warm and wet. She wiped at it. Her hand came away sticky.

Disoriented, forgetting what her mission had been or if she'd had a mission at all, she paused. What was she going to do? Couldn't remember . . . gotta remember. Something smart. Something clever . . . something important.

It would be so nice to just put her head down on the ground and go to sleep. But there was something she had to do first. If only she could remember.

She peered into the darkness. Nothing.

She listened.

Talking. Directly above her.

"Thanks for the help."

Brett.

"You wandered outside, fell down a hill, hit your head

on a rock, and died. Nobody will even ask any questions."

"Brett Gillette. Brett Gillette," she said in a singsong voice. "Pet, wet, net—"

"Stop it."

"Let Brett get met."

"I said, stop it!"

"Debt, set, get, fet. Oops. Not a word, not a word."

"Shut up!"

Less than a foot from her ear came a pop. That was followed by another. And another.

Now she remembered. What she had to do. What was so important.

She didn't want to touch him, but she had to.

She reached out and grabbed Brett's leg. Then, with her other hand, she reached in front of her, for the popping sound, and wrapped her fingers around the electric fence.

25

The cell door swung open.

Nathan was a free man.

Dressed in an institutional green shirt with the words Metamora County Jail stenciled across the back in large black letters, he ran down the dimly lit hall.

Trent wasn't slow. Nathan had to give him credit for that. It had only taken a couple of minutes to convince him that Lark was in danger and Nathan should be released.

Outside, Nathan remembered he didn't have his truck.

Shit.

He took a step in one direction, then the other.

Shit.

A patrol car pulled up to the curb.

Now what?

The passenger door opened and Trent looked up at him. "Get in. I'll give you a lift."

Under any other circumstances, Nathan would have told him to get screwed. But a killer was loose and Lark could be in danger. Without hesitation, Nathan got in.

Trent apparently felt the same sense of urgency. He put the car in gear and they cruised out of town. When they hit the highway, Trent tromped the accelerator and they roared down the road doing about ninety, both men silent.

It wasn't long before the bright headlight beams cut a path up the lane that led to Nathan's house.

There was Lark's car, the doors wide open. Nearby sat a big blue gas-guzzler.

"Gillette." Trent cut the headlights and crept to a stop some distance from the house. "What's he doing here?"

Nathan stared at the boat of a car, a sick feeling in his stomach. "He used to go out with Mary Jane." Dread weighed heavy in his voice, his heart.

"Son of a bitch," Trent said in a forehead-smacking tone. "I wanted you so bad I missed the obvious."

Now that the engine was off, Nathan could hear cattle bawling from the east pasture. Something was wrong.

Nathan reached for the door handle. "You take the house, I'll take the field."

"Wait." Trent leaned over and opened the glove compartment. "You'll need this." He handed him a flashlight. Then he grabbed a black leather holster, snapped it open, and slid out a pistol. "Know how to use it?"

Nathan shook his head. "No," he had to admit, even though he'd held a similar gun on Trent that very morning.

He got a quick lesson. "There's no safety. You just cock it like this, then pull the trigger." He checked the cartridge. "Six shots." He snapped it back into place and handed the weapon to Nathan.

It was cold. Heavy. Nathan didn't like it at all.

"Oh, and Nathan—"

Nathan stopped.

"I didn't touch her."

"I know." Nathan tested the weight of the gun in his hand. "Otherwise you'd be dead right now."

Then they were off, Trent moving silently in the direction of the house, Nathan the pasture.

Lark dragged herself across the ground.

Had to get away.

Had to keep moving.

She collapsed, resting her spinning head against the coolness of the wet grass. It felt so good to stop, felt so good to rest, to just let go.

Suddenly a hand wrapped around her arm.

Lark screamed, then gasped in pain as she was jerked roughly to her knees. Cruel fingers wrapped in her hair, pulling her head back.

"You bitch!" Brett tugged at her hair, almost ripping it out by the roots. "You shocked me!"

The voice didn't sound like Brett, not the Brett she knew. This was someone else.

This was the devil.

A madman.

Lark's scream chilled Nathan's blood. He slid the rest of the way down the steep embankment, dirt and pebbles skittering around him. When he reached the bottom, his heart stopped.

Illuminated in the strong beam of the government-issue flashlight was Lark.

On her knees.

Blood.

Everywhere. On her face. In her hair. Her white top was stained brown.

Gillette stood behind her, a fist in her hair, a knife to her throat.

Nathan froze.

Lark's earlier words came back to him: *He had a knife . . .*

Nathan wanted to charge, wanted to tackle Gillette to the ground. Wanted to kill him.

"Nathan." Lark hardly spoke above a pained whisper. "Go away. Please go away."

"That's right, Senatra. Go away." Gillette's voice was high-pitched, a man teetering on the edge. "She doesn't want you here."

There was no way Nathan could shoot the gun he held in his hand. Under the best of conditions, it would be risky. As it was, to fire was unthinkable.

"What are you doing, Gillette?" It was a struggle to keep his words level, under control when he really felt like shouting. "Why would you want to hurt Lark?"

"Because. *She* hurt *me.*"

"Lark wouldn't hurt anybody. This has nothing to do with her. Think about it, Gillette. It's me you really want."

"She cheated on me. She slept with you."

Lark's head lolled back, falling against Brett's thigh.

Nathan's heart jumped in fear. "Lark?"

She made a groggy sound. She tried to lift her head.

"Stay with me, honey."

"Don't call her honey. Try whore." He laughed, an eerie sound.

Nathan ignored him. "Are you with me?"

"Yes." Her voice was thick, groggy.

Running out of time. Had to think fast. Talk fast.

His mind raced as he desperately searched for something to say that would throw Brett off, that would distract him.

"Did you know Mary Jane was pregnant when you killed her?"

"What are you talking about?" Gillette asked, his voice thick with suspicion.

"She was pregnant."

Silence. Then, "You're lying."

Nathan heard the doubt in Gillette's voice.

"It's true. Trent just got the report back from the crime lab." He paused for effect. He paused to make sure Lark was conscious. "Mary Jane was pregnant." Now for the kicker. "You killed your own baby."

Gillette tilted his face toward the sky and let out an anguished sob.

"*No!*"

He released his hold on Lark. She fell facedown on the ground.

The next couple of seconds happened in slow motion. Nathan saw Brett reach for Lark. Saw the flash of a knife blade.

After that first hunting trip, Nathan had never wanted to hold a gun again. And now, here he was, holding one for the second time in a single day.

He squeezed the trigger. The shot rang out.

The stars were up there again. Lark could see them swirling, swirling.

Someone was bending over her, saying her name in a trembling, scared voice.

Nathan?

She must have fallen asleep, because it seemed just a heartbeat later that a light was shining in her eyes . . . she heard Nathan's quick intake of breath, heard him make a strange choking sound, almost like a sob.

She squeezed her eyes shut, trying to block out the glare, the intrusion reminding her of another time, another person. Had to get up. Had to run.

She struggled to get away.

Gentle hands held her down. "Lark. Don't move. You'll hurt yourself."

"Have to get away . . . have to, have to . . ."

From far away came a shout.

And then Nathan was answering back, calling over his shoulder. "Down here! Call an ambulance. We need an ambulance!"

Brett. He was going to kill her. Just like he'd killed Mary Jane. "He hurt me."

"I know, sweetheart." Nathan's voice was thick. He sounded as if somebody had hurt him, too.

"He can't hurt you now."

"Yes he can. He's here. Hiding. Listening."

"Shhh. He can't hurt you."

"He can. He killed Mary Jane. He wants to kill me."

"He's dead. Gillette is dead."

"D-dead?"

"Yes."

"How?"

"I killed him."

"Oh Nathan . . ."

Her fault. Her fault. Tears clogged her throat, choking her. Drowning. Pulling her down, down into the icy black water.

"C-cold . . ." she said through frozen lips. "S-so c-cold."

Another voice, vaguely familiar, saying something about an ambulance. "She's cold," Nathan said over his shoulder. "Get something to cover her."

She must have drifted off. A short time later she felt a blanket being tucked around her, the fabric scratchy against her skin.

"Nathan . . ."

"What, sweetheart?"

Why was he calling her sweetheart all of a sudden? And in that tone of voice?

She opened her eyes just a crack. The bright light was gone. Nathan was just a shadow against the stars. He leaned closer, and she whispered: "I like sheep."

"Sheep?"

For a moment, the blankness of his tone made her forget where this was going. Then she felt the rough fabric against her cheek. "But I . . . don't like . . . wool."

He laughed.

Or was it a laugh? It almost sounded like he was crying.

They took her away.

After carrying her up the hillside, they took her away.

He kissed her yellow blood-caked hair, touched her ashen cheek, then she was gone, loaded into the ambulance, the double doors closing behind her.

Nathan stood there on the hilltop, a breeze lifting his hair, watching two vehicles make their way across the pasture, one carrying Lark, the other the body of Brett Gillette.

You had to be careful this time of year. Driving through grass that had gone to seed was hell on a radiator.

A guy had to be careful.

"She'll be okay," Trent said, coming up behind him.

People always said that. They'd said that when his father had died, and when his mother had died.

Nathan bent over and picked up the gun he'd dropped. He stared at it, wondering how such a device had come about. How had somebody ever invented such a thing?

"Here." Trent took the weapon from him.

"I hate guns," Nathan told him.

"Me, too."

"Yeah, right."

"I do. I see them as a necessary evil. You did what you had to do. You saved Lark's life."

Nathan looked in the direction the ambulances had gone. A damp wind blew across his skin. Around him, the grass whispered. "I hope so. I sure as hell hope so."

"Go home. You look like hell."

"I'm going to the hospital."

Trent didn't argue, most likely knowing there would be no way to keep Nathan away.

Without stopping to change, Nathan got his truck and drove straight to Metamora County Hospital.

"Immediate family only," he was told at the desk. "We already notified her parents." The nurse looked at her watch. "They don't expect to reach here until early morning. She'll be out of surgery by then."

"Surgery?" God. He'd hoped for a concussion, a few stitches at the worst.

"We're waiting for the surgeon, Dr. Martha Francis, to arrive. We don't know for sure, but Dr. Bailey suspects a brain contusion. That means something will have to be done to relieve the pressure."

"Christ." Nathan closed his eyes and found the nearest wall to hold him up.

"You look like hell."

The voice came from Doc Bailey, who stood regarding Nathan, a rather pleased expression on his face. "Let me look at that shoulder." He lifted the neckline of Nathan's shirt.

Nathan winced. "What about Lark?"

"She's in good hands. Nurse. Bring an ice pack." That order was followed by one for a painkiller, and something Nathan would later suspect was a fairly potent sleeping pill.

The next thing Nathan knew, sunlight was streaming in the waiting room window, his neck hurt from sleeping with it bent, and the ice in the ice pack had melted and soaked into his shirt.

Off to his right and down a hall, he heard people talking in low voices.

He groaned and sat up, then shoved himself to his feet, careful to keep his bad shoulder immobile. Then he moved in the direction of the voices.

He heard something about hair, and about relieving the pressure. Then, "Your daughter is going to be fine."

"Oh thank God."

He looked around the corner to see an elderly couple, both with gray hair and matching beige slacks, talking to someone who must have been Dr. Francis.

Lark's parents. Older than he would have expected. Quietly refined.

"We tried to talk her out of coming here in the first

place," the mother said, fiddling nervously with the straps of her beige purse. "But she wouldn't listen."

"Not that we're interfering," the father added. "It's just that Lark . . . well, she's had trouble adjusting to the world. We worry about her."

The mother took up the story. "All of her friends have gotten married. Had children. But Lark, well, we just wish she could get over . . ."

Her words trailed off as Nathan made his appearance.

Dr. Francis took the opportunity to excuse herself. As her footsteps faded, Nathan suddenly found himself being regarded by a couple who looked as if they had somehow wandered into the wrong part of town. Their horror-filled gazes went from his hands, to his face, back to his hands.

He looked down—and saw the blood, Lark's blood, their daughter's blood—on his shirt, his jeans, his hands. Unconsciously, he touched his face, his fingers coming in contact with a jaw that hadn't seen a razor for a week.

And it occurred to him that he was everything and more of what they wanted to protect their daughter from. He was sure they wouldn't have welcomed his heartfelt confession.

I'm in love with your daughter.

He passed on the introduction, turned, and headed in the opposite direction.

From behind him came a gasp, then a loud whisper. "My God. A prisoner. A criminal. Loose in the hospital. Call the police!"

Too late, Nathan remembered his shirt with the words Metamora County Jail emblazoned across the back.

26

One week after leaving Lark's parents hysterically contemplating the back of his shirt, Nathan headed for the Metamora Mental Health Institute. It turned out that Lark had told Adam Trent everything about Nancy and her unborn baby. That it had been Gillette's, not Nathan's.

Years ago, Nathan had made a feeble attempt at the truth, beginning with his parents, but even they'd fallen for Nancy's story. She'd been very convincing. Nathan had felt so guilty over her attempted suicide that he hadn't pushed it. The less said, the better, he'd figured.

At the mental health building, he was told he could find Nancy Trent in the music room.

Walking down the hall, he heard the piano, slightly out of tune, being played one single, hesitant note at a time. Nancy had been fairly musical once. But that was years ago. Things change.

He stood in the doorway, hands in his pockets, waiting, watching.

Behind her was a picture window, the backlight making it hard to see her clearly.

She stopped playing and looked up, no surprise in her expression, only acceptance. She was old and she was young. Her face had retained some baby fat, the way people did when they hadn't lived an active, full life. Her eyes had wrinkles at the corners. Her hair, hair that used to be a shiny black, was streaked with gray.

He felt an incredible sadness.

"Hi, Nancy."

He stepped closer, his eyes fighting the contrast of light and shadow.

"Adam told me you were coming," she said.

He and Trent had talked about it. Trent had told him about Nancy's regrets, about how she wanted to see him, to apologize, and by so doing absolve herself.

"I want you to know I never hated you," Nathan said quietly.

She made a little hiccuping sound and looked away, down at the piano keys. "It's funny," she said, "but along the way, a strange thing happened. I started to believe my own lie. And as time passed, as more people told and retold my story, the more credence it had, and the more it seemed to be the truth."

"I never hated you."

"I heard about Mary Jane. I'm sorry."

"It wasn't your fault." Lately he'd come to realize that it hadn't really been Mary Jane's fault either. He hadn't loved her. He'd married her because he thought she was safe, somebody he couldn't hurt.

"If I hadn't lied, then maybe none of this would have happened."

"That was years ago. You were a kid. I was a kid. Kids

do dumb things. Adults do dumb things. It's human nature. Let it go."

But she seemed to need to talk about it. "I wanted to make you like me. Isn't that silly? You can't *make* somebody like you."

"I did like you. I do like you. Just not the way you had in mind."

She gave him a fragile smile.

"Adam says you might be getting out of here soon."

She sniffled and seemed to brighten. "I could walk out of here right now, but I'm not ready. I've been here a long time. I feel safe where I am. But I'm taking medicine that's really helping me. I'm better. Adam says whenever I'm ready, I can move in with him."

"That would be nice. Not just for you, but for Adam."

"Yes." She sounded thoughtful. "I think you might be right. He's been alone a long time too."

Nathan left her there, playing the piano. As he walked down the hallway, he heard her hit a wrong note, stop, then try again.

Lark's parents had spent the last week hovering anxiously over her, watching every breath she took, monitoring every bite of food she put in her mouth. She'd been horrified to find that they'd spent the first two days of her hospitalization sleeping on chairs in the waiting room. After that, one of the nurses had managed to talk them into moving into one of the empty rooms. The Metamora County Hospital wasn't a very busy place.

Her parents shouldn't be sleeping in chairs. It made Lark feel terribly guilty. They were getting on in years. *She* should be taking care of *them*.

But it turned out they'd made themselves at home,

her dad visiting with the patients, regaling them with bird stories. By the time Lark was ready to check out, her father had become quite a favorite with nurses and patients alike.

"It will be so nice to have you home," her mother told her. "Where you can sit in the garden and rest. I've seen some beautiful butterflies, and you should see the hummingbirds."

That's when Lark told her parents she had to go somewhere, had something to do before they left town. A final entry in her contented animal journal.

"You're driving?" came the horrified question.

Days ago, Nathan had driven her car to the hospital and dropped her keys off at the desk. But he hadn't come to see her. She'd finally quit looking for him to come. She'd finally understood that he wasn't coming.

"Yes, in the car."

"We'll take you."

"I really need to go by myself."

"All right, honey."

A hard thing for them to say, Lark realized.

Two pairs of anxious eyes stared at her.

"Don't worry about me."

"We won't."

They would. They would worry until she got back, until they knew she was once again safe.

Nathan peered at the bedside clock with sleep-blurred eyes. 9:00 A.M. Damn. He'd overslept again.

His days and nights were screwed up. He couldn't sleep. That was his problem. All night long he'd toss and turn and sweat. Just as the birds were starting to make noise, just as the sun was beginning to lighten the eastern sky, he'd fall into a restless sleep. And wake up late.

Now he scrambled out of bed, trying to ignore a headache brought on by lack of sleep. Without stopping for any kind of food, something else he hadn't been getting enough of lately, he headed outside.

And saw a small white car parked in his driveway.

His heart thumped oddly in his chest.

He thought she'd left, thought she'd gone back to California with her parents. His feet took him across the yard he still hadn't gotten around to mowing, up the dirt lane. When he topped the rise he saw her, sitting in the pasture with the cattle.

She was wearing what looked like the same flowered skirt he'd seen her in that first day. But now, instead of a sweater, she wore a sleeveless white top. On her head was a cream-colored cap, pulled down low. And dangly earrings.

He approached her, his feet stirring the grass, announcing his arrival.

She looked up from her notebook. "Nathan. Hi." As if nothing had ever happened. As if she'd just seen him yesterday.

She'd lost weight. There were dark circles under her eyes.

He was afraid for her. He wanted to wrap his arms around her, pull her up against his chest, and hold her tight.

"What are you doing here?" he asked, taking up his old role, the one he knew best. "I thought you were a quitter."

"Oh, I am." She smiled sweetly. "I've quit being a quitter."

"You're continuing with the study?" Suddenly a

strange electricity began pulsing through him, waking up his nerve endings.

"Actually, today is my last day. I'm making my final entries. Then we're catching a plane for California tonight."

"Ah." He nodded, his mind and emotions quickly shifting gears, his heart racing in panic.

"How come you didn't stop by to see me?" she asked.

He'd tried. But then he'd catch himself thinking about her parents, about how they'd reacted to him. "I thought it would be better if I stayed away."

"I waited for you."

"I'm sorry."

"I wanted to talk to you about what happened."

"I thought you'd want to forget about it."

"I can't. Can you?"

"No." He thought about it all the time, every second. "No."

"I want to thank you for saving my life."

He made an impatient sound and waved a hand to let her know it was nothing. If it hadn't been for him, her life would never have been in danger in the first place.

"And I wanted to tell you how sorry I am that you had to take a life to do it." Her voice caught. "Adam told me how you feel about guns."

So it was Adam now, not Officer Trent.

She looked away, but not before he saw her lips tremble, not before he saw the glimmer of tears in her eyes.

That was enough for him to let go of the act, the old Nathan. He dropped to one knee beside her. "Lark—"

He put a finger to her chin, lifted her head, bringing her gaze to connect with his. He started to tell her it couldn't have been helped, that it was either Gillette or her, but his thoughts trailed off. Her cap . . .

He let go of her chin and reached for the brim of her cap.

"No! Don't!" Both of her hands came up, stopping him, holding on tight.

"Lark. Let me see."

Her fingers fell away. She sat there braced, ready, hands at her sides.

He slowly pulled off the cap.

A sound of regret escaped him before he could stop it.

Her hair.

Her beautiful hair was gone. All that was left was a blond burr of half-inch stubble.

"Your hair . . ." was all he could say, staring.

"I thought you knew. I thought that's why you didn't come to see me."

He made a choking sound.

"It looks terrible," she said, quite clearly mortified. "but it will grow back."

On the top of her head, an inch past her hairline, was a red scar, not yet healed.

She could have *died*.

She let out a nervous laugh. "My dad says I look like a baby bird."

She was beautiful, he thought with astonishment. Even bald, she was beautiful. "You know, if the sun was just right—" He took her notebook, tossed it down, and pulled her to her feet. Holding her by both arms, he sidestepped her so the sun hit her at the right angle. Then he turned her just so—until a shaft of sunlight fell through the yellow hair on her head. "A halo. You have a halo."

She watched him, bemused, as he rubbed the palm of his hand lightly across the top of her head. "I like it."

"You're just saying that."

"No, I do. It feels neat."

"It does?"

"Yeah. Here—" He took her by the wrist, the bones beneath her flesh feeling incredibly fragile, scaring him all over again. "Rub your hand across it like this." He moved her hand back and forth. "Doesn't that feel weird. Weird, but nice?"

Concentrating on the sensation, she finally smiled, then agreed. "Yeah. Yeah, it does."

And then she started to laugh. But suddenly the laughter changed.

Suddenly she was crying.

And this time, he didn't stop himself. He pulled her into his arms, inhaling the scent of her, absorbing the feel of her against him, willing his strength into her. "Shh." He rocked her against him, trying to be strong, trying not to fall apart.

And then he was kissing her, gently, tasting the salt of her tears, her sorrow.

"Don't cry," he begged, his words spoken against her face, her cheek.

She pulled back enough to look up at him. Her eyes were swimming with tears. "Why didn't you tell me about your plants?"

"What?"

"The plants you were growing upstairs. I saw the marijuana poster. I just thought— why did you let me think you were growing pot?"

"The poster was left there by the last tenant's son. I never took it down." He shrugged. "It doesn't matter."

"It does. I threw away years of your life. And you didn't even say anything."

"You were already upset. You didn't need something else dumped on you. And anyway, I have more seeds. It won't be like starting over, not from the beginning anyway."

She sniffled. "All the while I was condemning you, you were being some silent hero."

He was going to miss her. He was going to miss her like hell. The pain of missing her was already a hollow spot deep inside him. He thought about her going back to California. Her parents would watch her. Take care of her.

In that instant, he understood what losing her meant. With Lark, his life could have been different. *He* could have been different. Better.

"California," he said. "It has earthquakes. And fires. And smog."

"It has the ocean," she said. "And beaches. And beautiful weather."

"The weather's not so great here. Too hot in the summer, too cold in the winter. But I've always thought the weather in California was too perfect. Almost artificial. No challenge to it."

"I've never seen snow." Her voice was wistful.

"What?"

"I've never seen snow. One Christmas, we went to visit relatives in Indiana. I hoped it would snow, but it didn't."

"I can't believe you've never seen snow." He would like to be around when she saw her first snowflake.

"What's it like here in the winter? Does the water freeze?"

"Enough to ice-fish for four months."

"Ice-fish? Really? How?"

"You drill a hole in the ice. Turn a bucket upside down to use for a chair. Drop a line in the hole."

"How wonderful."

"It's cold," he warned.

It was hard for people to adapt to the cold when they hadn't grown up with it. Their skin was too thin or something. "And dark. In the winter, it's dark by four. But at night, you can see every star in the sky."

"Every star?"

He nodded.

She grew quiet. He sensed that she was pulling herself together, gathering her thoughts, as if she had something she wanted or needed to say.

"I don't know why I came to Metamora County," she told him in a quiet voice. "You were right. I didn't know anything about livestock. Or about farming. Or about the Midwest. But something told me to come. And I came. And after I got here, I knew I should leave, but I couldn't. Even though nothing was working out, something told me to stay." She pulled in a shaky breath. "It was you. *You* are the reason I came. *You* are the reason I stayed."

"Lark . . ." It was a protest. He didn't want the blame, or the credit.

She put a hand to his lips and shook her head. "Most of my life I've been either hiding or running away. Then I came here—" She touched his jaw. Lingeringly, tenderly. "And met you." She shook her head and gave him a sad smile. "You healed me. All these years, I've been looking for you and I didn't even know it."

You healed me.

He kissed her palm. He closed his eyes. And when he opened them, she was staring at him, as if trying to memorize every line in his face, every strand of hair.

"Your eyes are the bluest eyes I've ever seen," she said, her sorrow an ache in his chest.

He could only stare, knowing he would never see her again, not knowing what to do about it.

She blinked, then bent and picked up her tablet.

"Did I pass?" he asked, indicating the notes she was hugging to her chest.

"Oh yes."

"Are my cattle content?"

"That too."

He put her cap back on her head.

"Good-bye, Nathan Senatra."

His throat was tight; he could hardly speak. "Good-bye," he croaked, not wanting to watch her go, unable to take his eyes from her as she turned and walked away.

This was it. If he let her leave, his life wouldn't be the same. The sun would rise, but it wouldn't shine with the same intensity.

She's never seen snow.

Her parents, in their attempt to protect her, had built a wall around her, sheltering her not only from the bad, but the good too.

He'd heard about butterfly collectors who kept chrysalides in total darkness so that the newly emerged butterflies would not see light. If they didn't see light, they wouldn't move around. If they didn't move around, they wouldn't damage their wings. That way, they could be perfectly preserved.

Lark was one of those butterflies.

"Lark!"

She stopped. She turned. She waited.

"Don't go."

The words came, haltingly at first—fear of her rejection, fear that he'd misunderstood everything she'd said, holding him back. "Don't leave. Stay here. With me."

She made a sound, a kind of sob of disbelief. And then she was charging across the grass toward him, running too fast.

"Slow down." He didn't know if he liked this love stuff. It hurt.

She didn't slow down. Instead, she hurled herself into his arms, almost knocking him off balance, showering his face with kisses while she laughed and cried at the same time.

Her cap tumbled backward off her head. Sunlight touched her hair, almost blinding him.

Nathan went with her to tell her parents. It wasn't as bad as Lark had feared. All along they'd suspected something of the sort. Her mother kept giving Nathan sidelong glances, as if trying to figure out where she'd seen him before. Nathan and Lark gave them a ride to the Des Moines airport, with Nathan leaving them alone as they made their tearful good-byes.

"Call us if you need us," her father said, giving her a careful hug. "Day or night."

"I will."

"Get your rest. Take your vitamins," her mother added as they announced last call for boarding.

"I will."

And then her parents were hurrying down the portable walkway. They turned the corner and were gone. And Lark was suddenly afraid that things were happening too fast.

They watched until the plane took off, watched until it was completely out of sight. And then they headed back for Nathan's.

"You're exhausted," he told her once they were home. "You need to sleep."

Lark was scared, suddenly unsure of herself. "Hold me."

He held her. And then he made love to her. The most tender, heartbreaking love.

"Why does it make me so sad?" she asked later, curled up against him as she tried to stay awake, tried to understand.

She thought he would laugh. Instead, he kissed her gently on the mouth, and said, "Because beauty and sorrow sometimes intertwine."

Something else to love him for.

Later she woke to the feel of Nathan's lips brushing her forehead. "Get up, sleepyhead."

She groaned and looked to the window. "It's still dark."

"I have something to show you."

"Can't it wait until morning?"

"No."

She got up.

Too tired to bother with underwear, she slipped into a pair of shorts and one of Nathan's T-shirts.

Downstairs, they climbed into his truck and headed east, up the lane, through a couple of gates, to a hilltop overlooking the piece of land where she'd first seen Nathan.

He cut the engine.

The eastern sky was just beginning to lighten.

"What am I supposed to be looking for?"

"Keep your eyes on the field."

Sunlight continued to lighten the sky. As she watched, the green below them seemed to move. Slowly, slowly, like a giant waking from a deep slumber.

Puzzled and captivated by the surreal drama playing out before her, Lark opened her door and slid from the passenger seat. Never taking her eyes from the moving field, she rounded the truck.

Behind her, a door slammed, then Nathan was beside her, taking her hand. She stared at the field until her eyes ached, until she finally understood.

Flowers.

Sunflowers.

Nathan's sunflowers.

The movement that had so perplexed her was the bending and turning of the huge yellow blooms.

"They follow the sun," Nathan explained.

"They're beautiful." Her voice was hushed, reverent.

She'd always dreamed of meeting a man who would give her flowers. He grew them. Acres and acres of flowers.

"By tonight, they'll be facing west again. I like to come out here just as the sun comes up. It's . . . I don't know. Kind of reaffirming," he added, as if a little embarrassed to admit his feelings in the bright light of day.

He was remarkable. After all he'd been through, he was still able to see with his eyes and feel with his soul. As long as he could look around and take pleasure in nature, then he would be okay.

"You're not crying, are you?" There was a bit of panic in his voice.

"No." She wiped at her eyes and her fingers came away wet. "Yes."

And then he asked her to marry him.

EPILOGUE

Nathan lay on his back on the front porch, his eyes closed, the warmth of the sun penetrating his flannel shirt, making him drowsy.

Something tickled the end of his nose. He opened his eyes to see his two-year-old daughter leaning over him, a dandelion in her hand.

He made a munching sound and pretended to eat the flower. Kaitlin giggled hysterically, as if she'd never seen him do anything like it before. He grabbed her and lifted her above his head while she shrieked in delight.

He put her back down.

Above their heads, a blue jay scolded them. Kaitlin pulled a wet finger from her mouth and pointed skyward. "Ellow bebbi saser."

"Yellow-bellied sapsucker?" Since her Grandfather Leopold's last visit, every bird she saw was a yellow-bellied sapsucker.

She nodded, then put the end of the dandelion to her pink lips—and took a drag.

"I see you've been to visit Grandma Millie," he said dryly.

"Gamma Mamma. Gamma Mamma." She laughed and started galloping in circles, her feet slapping the floor.

"You're wired."

"Wied. Wied."

Lark came around the corner of the porch. "Your grandmother slipped her some Mountain Dew."

"That explains everything."

Lark wore a sundress the color of ripe wheat. Her arms and legs were bare and tan. She approached him with an ornery smile. Then she straddled him, sitting down on his lap. Taken by surprise, he tumbled backwards, bringing her with him. She braced a hand on either side of his head, and leaned close, her shoulder-length hair brushing his face. "I think I'm ovulating," she whispered.

He slipped his hands up her dress, palms to her thighs, rubbing her delicate skin. "You always say that."

"I always want you."

His heart tripped. Truth was, he loved her so much it scared him. Here they were living in the same house he'd been living in when they'd met. The place was now insulated, with Kaitlin in what Nathan teasingly called the reefer room, his sunflowers moved downstairs and doing quite nicely in one half of the kitchen.

The seeds weren't yet perfected, but he was close. Very close.

How could Lark be happy stuck away in the sticks with a guy like him? But she seemed to be thriving. She didn't even seem to mind that he hadn't finished high school.

"You've accomplished more than most people with a formal education," she told him when he'd finally come clean on that issue. She'd actually seemed *proud* of him.

"Think Kaitlin will take a nap?" he asked hopefully.

"With all that sugar and caffeine in her?"

They both looked over at their daughter—who he now realized had grown very quiet.

She was sitting with her legs straight out, head resting against the porch railing, sucking her thumb, her eyes staring blankly ahead.

"I think she burned up her extra fuel on re-entry."

"I told your grandmother not to give her any pop, but the second I turned my back—"

"That's Grandma Millie for you. Just so she doesn't start supplying her with cigarettes."

To his regret, Lark released him, giving him a tanta-lizing glimpse of her panties. It was a little while before he could even think of getting up.

Recovering, he finally got to his feet. Moving quietly, he went over and picked up his daughter. "Come on, sweetheart." One chubby arm circled the back of his neck as she snuggled against him, her hair sweet and baby soft against his face.

"Book," she said, her long-lashed lids fluttering closed over the bluest eyes he'd ever seen.

"I'll read you a book." He pressed his lips to her brow. "How about *Baby Farm Animals*?"

"Moo."

He looked over her head. Lark was watching him, a tender smile on her face. His heart just kind of con-tracted. And in that second, he saw his life's path. This is where everything had led him.

All those years, he really hadn't known why he'd struggled so hard to defend the land, to fight for change, why he'd hung on against so many odds, so much ridicule.

Now, as he looked at the woman who meant the most to him in the world, as he held his sleepy daughter in his arms, he understood it all.